"Going once. Twice. And the winner is paddle fifty-eight. Alexandra Jamison."

There was a pause and then explosive applause. Once more Alexandra felt her gaze being pulled over to where Nathan Montgomery stood. He winked at her and then strode down the catwalk. Alexandra couldn't tear her eyes away, not blinking until he had disappeared behind the curtain.

Somewhere in the recesses of her mind, she heard Veronica announcing that the event had been an unqualified success. She then told the winners where they could pay their donation and meet their dates. Now that it was over, the rush from winning faded and Alexandra no longer floated on air. She'd landed back to earth with a thud as reality struck her.

She'd just bid a ridiculous amount of money to go on a date with a man she'd never laid eyes on before tonight.

Dear Reader,

Welcome back to Aspen Creek, Colorado, where love is once more in the air. This time love is coming for Nathan Montgomery and Alexandra Jamison.

Nathan has seen his two brothers fall in love, but he is clear that a relationship doesn't fit in his five-year plan. Alexandra has been burned by love and has no interest in a man. She is content to raise her infant daughter and leave romance for others.

Then Nathan's brother enters him in the Aspen Creek Bachelor Auction. Alexandra—egged on by her friends—wins a date with him. Although Nathan and Alexandra hit it off, they agree that the date is a one-time thing. You've probably already guessed that it doesn't work out that way.

I love writing about couples who are determined not to fall in love. It makes it that much sweeter when they do. I hope you enjoy reading *Wrangling a Family* as much as I enjoyed writing it.

I love hearing from my readers. Visit my website, kathydouglassbooks.com, and drop me a line. While you're there, sign up for my newsletter.

Happy reading!

*Kathy*

# Wrangling a Family

— 

## KATHY DOUGLASS

HARLEQUIN

**SPECIAL**
EDITION

# HARLEQUIN®

## SPECIAL
## EDITION™

Recycling programs
for this product may
not exist in your area.

ISBN-13: 978-1-335-59446-4

Wrangling a Family

Harlequin Enterprises ULC
22 Adelaide St. West, 41st Floor
Toronto, Ontario M5H 4E3, Canada
www.Harlequin.com

**Printed in U.S.A.**

**Kathy Douglass** is a lawyer turned author of sweet small-town contemporary romances. She is married to her very own hero and mother to two sons, who cheer her on as she tries to get her stubborn hero and heroine to realize they are meant to be together. She loves hearing from readers that something in her books made them laugh or cry. You can learn more about Kathy or contact her at kathydouglassbooks.com.

This book is dedicated with much love and appreciation to my husband and sons. Your love and support mean the world to me.

## Chapter One

"Let me stop you right there," Alexandra Jamison said, holding up a hand and shaking her head. She needed to stop her friends before they got carried away by this ridiculous idea. "The answer is no."

"Don't say no so fast," Veronica said, her fork suspended halfway between her plate of shrimp scampi and linguini and her mouth. "At least not until you hear the entire plan."

"I've heard enough to know that I don't want any part of it." Alexandra replied.

"Perhaps you don't understand," Kristy said. "Because if you did, you'd realize it made perfect sense."

"I did understand," Alexandra said. Kristy was a sixth-grade math teacher and Alexandra suspected she was about to use her spoon to diagram the plan on her napkin. "We all bought tickets to the Aspen Creek dinner and bachelor auction. Now Veronica wants me to bid on a bachelor."

"It's for a good cause. The money raised will support several local programs for youth and new programs at the library." Veronica Kendrick, the children's librarian, was normally levelheaded, so this loony idea was out of character.

"I have no problem attending," Alexandra agreed. "It's the bidding on a bachelor that I don't want to do."

"Why not?" Marissa asked. Marissa and Alexandra were both nurses at the local hospital. Marissa worked in the ICU and Alexandra worked in pediatrics. They'd become fast friends when Alexandra moved to Aspen Creek five months ago. Marissa introduced her to Kristy and Veronica, and they'd become friends too. They got together regularly for dinner and conversation. Their bimonthly girls' night out had started so normally that Alexandra hadn't expected this at all.

"It'll be fun," Kristy promised.

"How is bidding on some guy I don't know so I can spend the night with him *fun*?"

"You don't have to spend the night with him. It's just a date," Veronica said.

"You know what I meant. Besides, it'll make me look desperate." She hadn't uprooted herself and her child only to have that reputation follow her here. It had been bad enough back home, where someone had started the rumor that she'd gotten pregnant in order to trap her rich, former boyfriend. It hadn't been true, but that hadn't stopped the gossip from spreading like wildfire around the hospital where she worked.

"No it won't. It will make you look like a caring member of the community who appreciates the importance of contributing to charity," Veronica insisted.

"You'll look like someone who wants to have fun," Marissa added.

"And you don't have to bid on a stranger," Kristy added. "You can always bid on someone you know."

Alexandra frowned. "That's even worse. Can you imagine bidding on one of the doctors I work with? That would be too weird."

"So no doctors," Kristy said, making a note on a piece of paper that seemingly materialized out of nowhere.

"Why am I the only one who has to bid on someone?"

"I would love to participate, but I can't," Veronica said. "I'm the auctioneer. It would be hard to bid and conduct the auction at the same time."

"I suppose not," Alexandra conceded. She looked at Kristy and Marissa. "But what about you two? Neither of you has a steady boyfriend."

"So what? We have busy social lives and date quite a bit. You, on the other hand, only leave the house to work or meet up with us. This will give you the chance to go on at least one date."

"I'm not looking to get involved with anyone right now. I have my daughter to think about. Chloe needs all of my time and attention."

"Nobody is saying that you have to start a relationship. Just have dinner with a nice guy," Marissa said.

"And maybe go to a club," Kristy added, doing a little chair dance.

"That sounds okay in theory. But things have a way of getting complicated really fast. I'd rather not take that chance right now. I still think that you two should bid on someone. It sounds like fun. And it's for charity."

"Don't be so quick to say no. There won't be any complications. And we know plenty of men. Besides, we expect the bidding to go high," Marissa said. "We're going to have to pool our resources in order to win even one date."

"Really?"

"Yes. These aren't just any run-of-the-mill bachelors you'll be bidding on. These are some of the most eligible men in Aspen Creek. And from out of town too—a couple of the guys even live in Denver," Veronica said. As one of the coordinators, she would know.

"Didn't you even look at the list of participants I gave you at lunch yesterday?" Marissa asked.

Alexandra shook her head. "Why would I? The names wouldn't mean a thing to me. Not to mention that I had no intention of bidding."

While Alexandra was speaking, Kristy rummaged through her purse. Now she pulled out the flyer advertising the Aspen Creek Bachelor Auction, pushed Alexandra's empty plate aside, and set the paper in front of her. "I had a feeling that might be the case, so I circled the names of men you might be interested in bidding on."

"That was such a good idea," Veronica said, rolling her eyes. "Let's see who *you* think Alexandra would like."

"Let's not," Alexandra said. She could have saved her breath. Her friends were too busy looking at the flyer to pay much attention to her.

When Veronica squealed, "Oh no, you didn't," Alexandra couldn't help but glance over to see who they were talking about.

"Who?"

"Dr. Hunt."

"What's wrong with him?" Kristy asked. "I think he's cute."

"We know," Marissa said. "So why are you trying to set Alexandra up with your secret crush?"

"I don't have a crush on him, secret or otherwise. I just appreciate how gentle he is when I bring Twinkie in for his exam."

"Is Dr. Hunt your vet?" Alexandra asked.

Kristy nodded. "Yes. And he's a good one. Twinkie adores him. And you know how cats can be."

Alexandra was a dog person, so she had no idea. But she nodded anyway. "You do talk about him a lot. Maybe you should bid on him for yourself. I'm willing to contribute to the cause if you think he'll go for a lot of money."

"Don't listen to them," Kristy said, waving her hands. "I don't have a crush on him."

"Right," Marissa said, stretching the word over several syllables.

"Who else is on the list?" Alexandra asked, getting into the spirit despite herself. Besides, looking didn't hurt anything. And hearing about the different bachelors would help her to learn more about her neighbors.

"Oh, you really are interested," Kristy teased.

Aspen Creek, Colorado, was a resort town and a very close-knit community. Despite the fact that the population of the town grew significantly during the winter months as vacationers came to ski and participate in other outdoor activities, and less so during the warmer months when people came to fish and hike, the town still managed to keep its sense of community. That was one of the things that had appealed to Alexandra.

"Not really. I'm an outsider. I need these bits of information to get a complete picture of the people in town," Alexandra said quickly. She'd moved to town to help her great-aunt who'd injured her hip. Alexandra's parents wanted to move Aunt Rose in with them in their suburban Chicago home, but she wouldn't hear of it. She loved Aspen Creek and refused to leave the home she'd lived in all of her adult life. As a compromise, Aunt Rose allowed Alexandra and her daughter to stay with her and provide the care she needed. Since Alexandra had just ended a disastrous relationship and wanted to start over fresh, it was the perfect solution for both of them. A man—

even one that supposedly came with no strings—was not part of the plan.

"What can you tell me about him?" Alexandra asked, pointing at a random picture. He wasn't one of the ones that had been circled, and she wasn't any more interested in him than she was in the others, but she wasn't above gathering what information she could.

"That's Nathan Montgomery," Marissa said. "I still can't believe he agreed to enter."

"Why? Is he a selfish jerk?"

"Nothing like that. He's generous and supports all the fundraisers. It's just that Nathan's all work and no play. There is no room in his life for anything other than his family's ranch. I would expect him to write a check and be done with it."

"So he's the serious type." Someone who wasn't interested in a relationship was the type of man she'd want to bid on. Not that she was going to bid on anyone.

"That's putting it mildly," Marissa said. "And not at all the type of man I would choose for you. Now Party Marty would be a better fit."

"Party Marty," Kristy said with a smile. "I agree. He would be better."

Veronica nodded. "He'll definitely show you a good time."

A guy named *Party Marty* couldn't be further from what Alexandra wanted. "No. I don't think so."

"So who are you going to bid on?" Veronica asked.

"I told you, I'm not bidding on anyone. I'll be happy to watch the auction." Alexandra took a breath and said firmly, "I'm really not interested in going out with anyone."

"Even though there is no second date? No commitment?" Kristy asked, clearly disappointed.

"Even then. I have enough on my plate right now. So, it's a no for me." Alexandra handed the flyer back to Kristy. "I won't be bidding on anyone."

Nathan Montgomery grabbed the crumpled flyer advertising the Aspen Creek Bachelor Auction from his back pocket and held it out to his brother Isaac, so that he could read it. Nathan barely reined in his anger. This nonsense had Isaac's fingerprints all over it.

"What's that?" Isaac asked without looking at it.

"It's a flyer advertising the bachelor auction."

"And why are you showing it to me? I certainly have no interest in it."

"I thought you might find one of the names particularly interesting."

Isaac dropped the saddle he'd been about to place on his horse, snatched the paper from Nathan, and began frantically searching it. "I'm not on here, am I? Savannah is laid-back, but I don't think she would appreciate me going out with another woman, even if it is to raise money for charity."

Savannah was Isaac's fiancée and one of the sweetest people Nathan had met. She'd suffered the loss of her first husband and child and had found happiness with Isaac. Nathan looked at his brother, his suspicion temporarily suspended. "Are you saying you didn't do this?"

"Do what?"

"Enter me in the bachelor auction."

"What? No. Why would I do something like that?"

"As a joke."

"Again, no. Although I have to admit the idea of you strutting your stuff down the catwalk is kind of funny."

"You think so? Well, I don't. I am not interested in anything to do with this shenanigan. But if you didn't do this, who did?"

"Maybe your name was added as a mistake."

"And my picture? No way. Somebody had to intentionally put me on the list."

"Good point. But instead of accusing innocent people, why don't you just call the person in charge and ask how you were added? There's a number right on the flyer."

"Good idea."

"I'm more than just a pretty face and great body." Isaac winked and then flexed, striking a pose. Despite his annoyance, Nathan laughed. Of the three Montgomery brothers, Isaac, the youngest, had gotten the majority of the charm, which had made him popular with the single women of Aspen Creek. Nathan didn't envy him though. He had goals that charm wouldn't help him accomplish. His serious nature and willingness to do the hard work was what had him in line to run the Montgomery Ranch when his father retired. Those qualities might not be what women were looking for, but they were going to help him make the business even more successful than it was now.

Right now, theirs was the biggest beef ranch in the state and enjoyed a superior reputation. But Nathan was eyeing more than Colorado or even the Midwest. Over the next five years, he wanted to expand the operation until they distributed their organic beef across the entire United States.

Being a rancher was in Nathan's blood. From the time he could walk, he'd followed his father around, mimicking everything he did. Nathan learned the business from the bottom up. He'd cleaned stalls, fed cows, participated in cattle drives, and arranged for the stock to be taken to market. The only time he hadn't lived on the ranch had been when he'd gone away to Howard University, earning first his bachelor's and then a master's degree in business. Although he'd enjoyed his time at college, he'd itched to return home to Colorado. Now, unless he was on a business trip or on a weekend getaway, he was on the ranch.

Nathan made a mental note to contact Veronica Kendrick when they were finished moving the cattle from their current grazing site to another. "I wonder what's keeping Miles."

"Probably Jillian or the kids. Besides, we aren't supposed to leave for another five minutes, so technically he's not late."

Nathan nodded. He knew that was true, but he liked to have everything in order ahead of time, just in case an issue arose at the last minute. He didn't like surprises.

"Hey," Miles called, jogging into the stable and heading for his horse. In a minute he'd saddled it and ridden up beside them. He looked at the flyer Nathan was still holding. "Oh, I see you have that. Good. With all of the busyness surrounding the wedding arrangements, I forgot to mention it to you."

"You're the one behind this?" Nathan's fist clenched, crushing the flyer.

"Yes. Is there a problem?"

"You have to ask? Of course there's a problem. Why in the world would you enter me in this ridiculous bachelor auction?"

"If you recall, you had me start attending those Chamber of Commerce meetings. They are such a waste of time. I agreed to go *once* because I was grateful that you babysat the kids so I could spend more time with Jillian. That one time morphed into me going every month."

"And I appreciate you taking that task off my plate."

"You say that as if I had a choice."

"So…what? This is your petty payback? Instead of coming to me with your issue like a man, you signed me up for this bachelor auction?"

"It wasn't like that," Miles objected.

"We all have to do our part to keep the ranch running. It is a *family* business. And the last time I checked you were part of the family."

"The ranch means as much to me as it does to you. And no, this isn't payback. When I have a problem with you, you'll know. But when I mentioned the fundraiser, you didn't let me go into detail. You just said that it was important that Montgomery Ranch be represented in a very visible way. To show that even though we are not geographically a part of Aspen Creek, that we are a part of the town in spirit. That whatever matters to the town matters to the Montgomery family."

Miles was quiet by nature, so this long speech was out of character. And unnecessary. Nathan wound his hand in a "get to the point" gesture. They had a schedule to keep.

"Well, Nathan, the fundraiser is this ridiculous bachelor auction. It was Deborah Lane's idea. But it quickly won the support of most of the women at the meeting. A few of the men even thought it was a good idea and signed up for it on the spot." He shook his head. "They decided to contact the single men in town to see if they were willing to participate. Apparently quite a few were."

"Nobody contacted me." He would have shut down that foolishness in a minute.

"That's because when they asked me if one of the Montgomery men was willing to participate, I said yes. Clearly I'm out. I'm getting married in three weeks. And Isaac is out because he's engaged. That left only you."

"You could have said no."

"Oh, how short your memory is, dear brother. The last time I said no about a fundraiser, you jumped all over me because I made the ranch look like a poor neighbor. I believe your exact words were *always say yes, Miles. Always.*"

"I remember that," Isaac said, not being the least bit helpful. But then, knowing Isaac, he hadn't intended to be. He delighted in being annoying. It was his superpower.

Nathan recalled the conversation too, although he wasn't going to admit it now. "And somehow you took that to mean I wanted to be bid upon like a cow?"

"Don't turn this on me. I was just following your blanket order. If you want to back out, then that's on you."

"Oh, come on. Why would he want to back out?" Isaac asked. "This is the stuff dreams are made of."

"How do you figure?" Nathan asked. Even Miles looked interested in Isaac's reply.

"Dozens of women willing to spend their hard-earned money for a chance to go out with you. What man wouldn't love that?"

*Me*, thought Nathan. *I wouldn't.*

But he and Isaac were different. Before Isaac had met Savannah and fallen head over heels in love, his nickname had been Isaac "love 'em and leave 'em happy" Montgomery. He'd dated nearly every woman in town, somehow managing to remain on good terms with all of them.

Nathan had never been as popular with the women as Isaac. But then, nobody was. Being a ladies' man wasn't among Nathan's goals. Not that he was opposed to relationships. They had their place. And time. And now wasn't the time for him to become involved with anyone. The ranch kept him busy and he wouldn't be able to give a woman the attention she deserved.

Not that he hadn't tried on more than one occasion. His last relationship had been a colossal failure. Janet had been a single mother of a six-year-old. He and Billy had been wrecked when the relationship ended, and Billy and his mother had moved to Iowa. But Nathan had learned his lesson—no dating single mothers.

There was an order to things. First he would establish the ranch as the premiere beef ranch in the nation. Then—and only then—would he look for a woman to share his life.

He didn't see what the big rush was to find a woman and get married anyway. After all, he was only thirty years old. There was plenty of time for a relationship in the future.

He'd explained himself to his brothers and parents several times, but they didn't understand. He wasn't going to waste his breath saying it again. "I don't want to lead anyone on."

"Lead them on how? They're bidding on one night. Dinner and maybe some dancing. Or a movie or concert. Nobody is expecting a marriage proposal. Or even a second date," Isaac said.

"Really? If that's all they want, why would they spend all that money for one date?"

"You got me," Miles said. "The whole idea is silly to me. There are plenty of other ways to support a charity. Like writing a check."

"Because it's fun," Isaac said. "You two really are sticks-in-the-mud. I can't believe we're related. Let me break it down for you. Not every date has to lead to a relationship. Sometimes people do things just for the sheer pleasure of it. Like bid on a date at a bachelor auction. Don't read more into it than is there."

"When did you get all logical?" Nathan asked. "You're actually making sense."

"I don't want to be out here all day. Savannah and I have plans for the evening, so I don't have time for you to have an existential crisis over something that doesn't matter. Take the winner to dinner and take her home. Thank her for her time and her charitable donation, and leave. Easy."

"Right?" Miles agreed. "What's the big deal? And it will generate goodwill for the ranch. That's something that's important. If you back out, we'll lose that goodwill and maybe even stir up some bad blood."

"And you definitely don't want to do that," Isaac said.

"No." That was the last thing he would ever want. The ranch was everything.

"Good. Now that it's settled, let's get this show on the road," Isaac said, leading the way from the stable, Nathan and Miles behind him.

As he rode out to the pastures beside his brothers, Nathan tried to convince himself that it was going to be as easy as Isaac claimed.

But he had a sneaking suspicion that the auction was going to be much more complicated than that.

## Chapter Two

Alexandra stepped into the ballroom and then looked around. The decorating committee had outdone themselves with red, pink, and white roses in marble vases. Enormous crystal chandeliers hung from the twenty-foot ceiling, illuminating the spacious room. There was a buzz of energy in the air, and despite telling herself that she really didn't want to bid on anyone, excitement built up inside her.

She spotted her friends at their table. She'd left work a few minutes later than scheduled and had needed to rush home in order to get dressed. Although she hadn't planned to make a big deal of this, she'd bought a new dress and shoes for the night. It had been a while since she'd been shopping, and she'd gone a bit over budget. But looking at the other women dressed in their designer finery and showy jewelry, she was glad that she'd done it. She knew that she looked good in her sleek black dress and heels.

Her friends had a table in a prime location near the end of the catwalk—probably because of Veronica's position as the auctioneer—and she made her way over to them.

"We thought you had backed out," Marissa said, rising to give Alexandra a hug.

"No. I got caught up at work."

"That's what your aunt said when I called, but we figured she was covering for you."

"Aunt Rose? No way. She tried to convince me to bid on a guy." Aunt Rose might be in her late sixties, but she had a very young attitude and was up for anything. Including parachuting out of a plane with her partner in crime, Bella Stewart, which is how she'd injured her hip.

Alexandra sat in a chair and looked around. "So where are the eligible bachelors?"

"They're here. They're eating dinner, same as us."

"Don't tell me that they have dates."

"I have no idea," Marissa said. "Why would that matter to you? You aren't bidding on anyone."

"Unless you changed your mind," Kristy said hopefully.

"No. I'm still not bidding," Alexandra said firmly. "But I'm willing to contribute to the cause. I just wanted to get a peek at the men before the bidding started."

"You won't have to wait long," Veronica said. She

glanced at her watch, then stood. "I'm about to get the auction started."

"Good luck," Alexandra said.

Veronica smiled and then winked. "I was made for this."

Veronica took her place behind the podium and a hush immediately came over the room. "Welcome to the first and hopefully not last Aspen Creek Bachelor Auction."

There was a roar and applause, and Veronica smiled as she waited for silence before continuing, "I am Veronica Kendrick, your host for the event. Before we start, I want to remind you that tonight's auction is raising funds for charity. Specifically, funds for children in underserved communities as well as children's programming at the library. So, ladies, raise those paddles, open up your wallets and get ready to bid. I guarantee you'll get your money's worth. Our sixteen bachelors will each walk the catwalk, so you'll get a chance to meet them all before the bidding begins. Now, without further ado, let the auction begin."

Nathan stood backstage and looked at the other bachelors. They were all laughing and talking among themselves, as if being paraded in front of the entire town was a good thing. Nathan knew a lot of them, counted a few among his friends, but he didn't feel at ease enough to engage in conversation. Although he'd had time to get used to the idea of participating in the auction, he still couldn't shake the feeling that he was making a big mistake.

He knew all of the benefits that would result from the auction and had reminded himself of them repeatedly since he'd discovered he was a participant. Money would be raised for charity. Although the town was well off, there were always needs to be met. People to help. He was all for that.

And there was the goodwill that the ranch would accrue. Not only in Aspen Creek, but in the state as well. Nathan wanted to take the business nationwide, which required him to make contacts. He wasn't convinced that this was the best way to bring attention to the ranch, but backing out would definitely do harm to their reputation, something he would never tolerate.

"You don't look like you're expecting to have fun," a man said, approaching Nathan.

"Is this supposed to be fun?" Nathan replied.

He grinned. "That's how I was sold on it."

"Sounds like you talked to my brother, former most eligible bachelor of Aspen Creek."

"Former?"

"He's engaged now."

"Don't say it like it's a life sentence."

"I'm not opposed to commitment. Just not now." He held out his hand. "I'm Nathan Montgomery, by the way."

"I know. I grew up here. I guess you don't remember me."

Nathan gave the other man a long stare. He'd prided himself on his memory, but it was failing him now. Still…there was something familiar about the guy, but

Nathan couldn't place him. "Sorry. I feel as if I should know you, but I can't recall your name."

"That's okay. I look a little bit different these days. I'm Malcolm Wilson."

"No kidding? You look a *lot* different. The Malcolm I remember was a short, scrawny guy."

Malcolm grinned. "I'm what my mother refers to as a late bloomer. I grew over a foot my freshman year in college and put on fifty pounds of muscle."

"What brings you back to town after all these years?"

He was a little hesitant. "It was time for me to come home."

Nathan nodded. "Well, this is certainly a way to make your presence known."

"So you haven't heard any talk about me?"

"Should I?"

"I don't know. If there's one thing I remember about Aspen Creek, it's that people like to speculate and gossip. My family owned a small ranch. I figured people are wondering what I plan to do with it."

"It's possible that they are. I don't live in town, so much of the news doesn't reach me. Besides, I don't gossip, so nobody would approach me with that kind of talk. But hey, welcome home."

"Thanks."

The backstage coordinator, Evelyn Parks, entered the room and clapped her hands. She was a member of the Aspen Creek Chamber of Commerce and the main reason there was always so much conflict at meetings. "It's time. You'll each be given a number.

When it is called, you'll walk on stage. Walk down the catwalk and then return to the stage and line up. Across, so that everyone will have a good look at you. Then you all will exit and return backstage, waiting until your number is called to be bid on."

"Showtime," Malcolm said, patting Nathan on the shoulder before going to get a number.

Nathan put on the cowboy hat he had been holding. He'd wanted to dress in black jeans, a white shirt, and his cowboy boots, but Isaac had nixed the idea. His brother had reminded him that the auction was for charity, and that he had to look his best to get the most money. So now Nathan was wearing a black suit, black shirt, and dress shoes.

"You don't intend to wear that hat, do you?" Mrs. Parks said, her tone of voice making it clear what she thought of the idea. Her snooty attitude only hardened his position.

"I absolutely do," Nathan said. He might have left his cowboy boots under his bed, but the hat was non-negotiable. No hat, no Nathan. "I'm a rancher."

"But you look so nice without it. And my Melanie is here and plans on bidding on you. You don't want your hat to turn her off, do you?"

Nathan managed to suppress a shudder. He and Melanie had been classmates. They'd never gotten along but over the years they had managed to keep their distance. Then one day, for a reason known only to herself, Melanie decided that the two of them would make a good couple. He'd done his best to disabuse her of that notion, but clearly he hadn't been successful. Ever since he'd realized that he couldn't back out of the auction, he had tried to put the upcoming date out of his mind. He hadn't considered the possibility that the winner might be someone he found completely unlikable. He could only hope that Melanie didn't win.

"I'm wearing my hat. Not only in the auction, but on the date as well." That last bit was a bluff, but she didn't need to know that.

Mrs. Parks compressed her lips and stalked away, her wide back stiff. Another volunteer handed Nathan an eight-by-ten cardboard with a number on it and then wrote Nathan's name on a clipboard. Wouldn't you know it? Nathan was number sixteen. He would be the last bachelor. He didn't know if that was good or bad. Maybe the women would have run out of money by then and he would go home by himself. A reject. Embarrassed before the entire town.

Nathan shook his head. He didn't want to date anyone, so why did the thought bother him? Besides, going last could be good. They would be building up to him. If he had the charm and magnetism of Isaac, he might believe that to be the case instead of what it actually was. He'd been talking to Mrs. Parks and had been the last person given a number.

He noticed that Malcolm was standing three people ahead of him. As the men walked onto the stage, there was a burst of applause and some cheers.

The things he did for the ranch.

He just hoped the whole mess would be over soon.

\* \* \*

Alexandra watched as the men walked onto the catwalk as their numbers were called, in what was intended to be the teaser before the auction started. Even subtracting the handful of outsiders, it was hard to believe that this many good-looking men lived in this pleasant resort town. And yet, each man who crossed the stage was even more handsome than the one before.

"Dr. Trevor Hunt," Veronica announced, breaking into Alexandra's thoughts. A handsome man in his early thirties stepped onto the stage and Alexandra sneaked a look at Kristy. She was staring at him like Alexandra stared at chocolate. Her friend might try to deny it, but it was clear that she was attracted to the veterinarian.

"You should totally bid on him," Alexandra said to Kristy.

"No way. He's my cat's vet. That would make things awkward between us."

"On the other hand, he might appreciate being bid on by a friend instead of a stranger."

"Do you think all of the women here are strangers? Granted, a lot of them have come in from out of town, but most of them live in Aspen Creek. Believe me, plenty of them will be bidding on him, so it's unlikely he'll end up with someone he doesn't know."

"If it's all right with you, it's all right with me."

"It is."

Alexandra turned her attention back to the stage, watching as the men continued to cross the stage.

Finally they got to the last man, who Veronica introduced as Nathan Montgomery. Alexandra had only seen him on the flyer the other day. The picture had been small, and it had been difficult to make out his features beneath his cowboy hat. Truthfully, she hadn't tried all that hard to see what he looked like. Now curiosity was getting the better of her.

And then he strode onto the stage as if he owned the place.

Alexandra took one look at him and barely managed to catch the gasp before it escaped her lips. The man was absolutely gorgeous. Dressed in all black, he had the best body Alexandra had ever seen. Even beneath his suit jacket, his broad, powerful shoulders were unmistakable. His well-formed chest tapered down to a trim waist. There was no disguising the muscular thighs of his long legs. He walked down the catwalk with confident strides. When he reached the end, he tipped his cowboy hat at the audience, eliciting cheers before turning and walking away.

Alexandra let out a sigh, glad that she hadn't swooned in front of her friends.

"What do you think?" Marissa asked, elbowing Alexandra out of her trance.

Alexandra smirked. "He's all right, I guess. If you go for that kind. He's a solid six."

"Right," Marissa replied, clearly not fooled. "Too bad you aren't going to bid on anyone."

The bachelors made their way backstage as the crowd applauded.

Bachelor number one remained on the stage. The

bidding started at one hundred dollars. In two minutes of fast and furious bidding, that sum had risen to six hundred dollars. And women were still raising their paddles, going even higher.

Finally the bidding stopped at seventeen hundred and seventy-five dollars. *Wow.* Somebody really wanted to win a date with him. Alexandra turned to Kristy. "Is he someone important?"

"What do you mean?"

"I mean is he a big shot? A politician? A millionaire?" When her friend only stared at her, she continued. "He went for a lot of money."

"Oh, that's Marty Adams. He owns a restaurant in town. He also has a brand of barbecue sauce that's sold in stores across the country."

In that moment, it clicked. "That's Party Marty?"

"Yes. The woman who won a date with him is going to have a fantastic time."

"So all of the bachelors aren't going to go for that much?"

Kristy laughed. "I doubt it. Why? Have you changed your mind about bidding? There are lots of good men available."

"And we'll contribute if that's what is holding you back," Marissa added. "After all, it's for a good cause."

"I know. The library."

Marissa leaned in. "And getting you to go on a date."

Alexandra only shook her head. She wasn't sure getting her on a date was worth that much money.

The bidding didn't slow as the night progressed.

In fact, the excitement built with each man and Alexandra was swept up in it. The energy had practically reached a frenzy by the time the last bachelor sauntered down the catwalk. Nathan Montgomery. His cowboy hat was fixed in a way that partially obscured his face. But what she could see of his handsome profile was enough to make her blood race. His brown skin was so perfect, she wondered if he got regular facials. That ridiculous thought didn't last a minute before she shooed it away.

From his confident and slightly irritated stance, and the way he commanded the room, it was clear that Nathan Montgomery was a man's man. The type who would never have a facial because he was too busy with more important things. Business? She wasn't sure, but he definitely didn't seem the type to be in this auction, no matter how good the cause.

She clenched the paddle that had sat unused on the table throughout the auction.

Marissa raised a questioning eyebrow.

"I'm just testing it out," Alexandra said weakly.

Kristy and Marissa laughed.

"There's no shame in bidding," Kristy said. "After all, the money will go to help kids."

Alexandra held her paddle in her lap as the bidding began. It started slowly and she wondered if the other women in town knew something about Nathan Montgomery that she didn't. Suddenly she felt sorry for him. He had pride just as much as she did. She knew what it was like to be embarrassed.

When the bidding stalled at five hundred dollars,

a respectable number although lower than the other bids, Veronica spoke from the podium. "Do I hear five-fifty?"

"Seven hundred dollars," someone called in a smug voice, as if she'd knocked out all of the other competitors and knew it.

"Will anyone go higher? Do I hear seven-fifty?"

Nathan Montgomery turned slowly on the runway and looked in her direction. Although she couldn't see his eyes under the brim of his Stetson, she practically felt his gaze burning into her own. Her skin began to tingle and she jumped to her feet.

"Seven-fifty," Alexandra called, as she raised her paddle.

"I guess you want him after all," Kristy said with a smirk, as Alexandra sat again.

"One thousand dollars," that annoying voice called.

"Eleven hundred," Alexandra said firmly before turning to her friends. "Who is that bidding against me?"

"That's Melanie Parks. She was Nathan's nemesis for years. You can't let her win," Kristy said. "Nathan deserves better than her."

"That's right. This is war," Marissa said, then jumped to her feet. "Twelve hundred dollars!"

"You just bid against me," Alexandra said, poking her friend in the side.

Marissa clapped her hands against her mouth and sank into her chair. "Sorry! I got carried away."

There was silence.

"Anyone else have a bid?" Veronica asked.

Alexandra shot Marissa a look and then bid. "Twelve hundred and fifty dollars."

After a short silence, Veronica spoke again. "Going once. Twice. And the winner is paddle 58. Alexandra Jamison."

There was a pause and then explosive applause. Once more Alexandra felt her gaze being pulled over to where Nathan Montgomery stood. He tipped his cowboy hat at her and then strode down the catwalk. Alexandra couldn't tear her eyes away, not blinking until he had disappeared behind the curtain.

Somewhere in the recesses of her mind, she heard Veronica announcing that the event had been an unqualified success. She then told the winners where they could pay their donation and meet their dates. Now that it was over, the rush from winning faded and Alexandra no longer floated on air. She'd landed back to earth with a thud as reality struck her.

She'd just bid a ridiculous amount of money to go on a date with a man she'd never laid eyes on before tonight. What had she been thinking? Why had she spent so much money?

And on a *date*? That was the last thing she should be doing right now.

"Wow. You did it. You bid on a bachelor," Kristy said, grinning broadly.

"I wasn't sure you would," Marissa said. "Especially since you were so set against it."

Alexandra wasn't sure if she was in shock, but she couldn't bring herself to move. Or breathe. Or anything else. "I was a bit surprised myself. But I guess

I finally got sucked into the action. And look at me now," she said weakly. "The winner!"

"Well, don't just sit there. Go pay and meet your date," Kristy said.

Alexandra nodded as she stood up, grabbing her purse. "I'll be right back."

"I feel as if I should contribute something," Marissa said, opening her purse. "After all, I did kick the price up by a couple of hundred dollars."

"You pay for my dinner next time we go out and we'll call it even," Alexandra said. When she and Owen had broken up, she'd sold most of the expensive jewelry that he'd given her. She hadn't wanted a reminder of how easily he'd turned her head. And of how wrong she'd been about him. But there was no way she was giving even one earring back to him. This wasn't exactly how she'd planned to spend the money, but a petty part of her that she rarely indulged reveled in the knowledge that Owen was funding her first date with another man since their breakup.

By the time Alexandra reached the cashier, there was no one in line. Alexandra set her paddle on the table and gave her name to the volunteer. A woman standing near the table shot Alexandra a dirty look before stomping away.

"Pay no attention to her," the cashier said. "Melanie is just upset that you outbid her."

"Oh." So *that* was Melanie. Alexandra slid her credit card into the reader and then approved the amount.

"Your cowboy is waiting," the cashier said, gesturing to where Nathan Montgomery stood. There were a couple of other bachelors nearby, but they were talking to other women. Veronica was standing close to one of the bachelors, engaged in what looked like a heated discussion. "Go introduce yourself to Nathan. Thank you for your donation. And have a great date."

"Thank you." Suddenly Alexandra felt shy, which was ridiculous. There wasn't a shy bone in her body. But experience was trying to teach her to think before she acted. Something she clearly had yet to learn. She'd just impulsively outbid a woman for a date with a man she wasn't sure she wanted to go out with simply because he'd looked divine in a cowboy hat. Well, there were no givebacks, so she needed to move ahead.

Inhaling deeply, Alexandra walked over to Nathan Montgomery.

"Hi," she said.

"Hi." He removed his hat and held it in his hands in front of him. She had the feeling that he didn't remove his hat often. "It appears that you have won a date with me."

"Yes." He'd spoken a bit stiffly and Alexandra was consumed with doubt. Had he hoped some other woman would win? "I hope that's all right with you. I ran into Melanie Parks at the table and she seemed a bit upset with me. If there's something between you two that I'm not aware of, I can always bow out."

"Absolutely not," Nathan said, immediately. "We are definitely not dating. We don't even run in the same circle of friends. Believe me, I am happy that you won the bidding war."

Alexandra smiled. She was relieved although she wasn't sure why. "Okay."

They stood there staring at each other. Clearly neither one knew what the next step should be. Since she was the one who'd won, perhaps the onus was on her to take the lead. She sighed. "I've never done anything like this before, so I'm at a loss as to what to do next."

"Why don't we sit down at one of the tables and figure it out?"

She nodded. Now that the auction was over, people were beginning to leave, so there were several empty tables to choose from.

Nathan held out his arm, allowing her to precede him. As she passed by him, she inhaled and got a whiff of his cologne. It was subtle and outdoorsy. She'd never smelled it before, but it was on the way to becoming her new favorite scent. She bypassed two tables and found one near the corner of the room, where they would have a bit of privacy. Nathan held out a chair for her and she sat. Once she was comfortable, he took a seat across from her. There were a couple of empty glasses on the table and he pushed them aside.

"You know my name, but over all of the applause, I couldn't make out yours."

"It's Alexandra Jamison. I'm new to Aspen Creek. I'm a pediatric nurse."

"Nice to meet you, Alexandra. I guess you already know a bit about me."

"Not really."

"You didn't read my biography on the flyer?" He

lifted one side of his mouth in a wry smile that she found oddly appealing and that had her stomach do a little flip-flop.

"Well, to be honest, no. I had no intention of bidding at all. My friends kind of egged me on and here we are."

"So… It was spur of the moment?"

"Yes."

He smiled and a dimple flashed in his cheek.

Their eyes met and she felt the same tingling sensation she'd experienced when he'd glanced at her from the runway.

"Are you sure there's no woman waiting in the wings."

"Positive. I don't date much, to tell you the truth. Now my brother Isaac on the other hand? All he has to do is breathe and women fall at his feet."

"You must have some fans. After all, you went for a lot of money."

He smiled. "Only because your friend jumped in."

Alexandra laughed. "She told me that she got caught up in the moment."

He threw back his head and laughed. The sound was robust and merry. "Perhaps you should have a talk with her about her emotions. If that keeps up, she could cost you a lot of money in the future."

"Well, since I don't plan on bidding on another man, I'm safe." She looked at him. "If you plan on doing this again, you're going to be at the mercy of some other woman. Like Melanie."

"Trust me, this was a onetime thing."

"You sound so definite."

"That's because I am. My brother is the one who signed me up. I only found out about it after the flyers had gone out. It would have looked bad for me to back out."

"Oh. Then maybe you need to have a talk with your brother," she said. "Otherwise you might become a regular attraction."

He smiled and butterflies fluttered in her stomach. Where had they come from?

"You're okay, Alexandra. This date just might turn out to be fun after all."

"I was just thinking the same thing. So, where would you like to go?"

"You just spent a lot of money, so you should decide."

"I don't know many places. If you don't mind, how about you make a few suggestions and we decide after that?"

"I can do that."

He reached into his inside jacket pocket and pulled out his cell phone. "If you want to give me your number, I'll call you. Then we'll both have each other's numbers."

She nodded and then reeled off her telephone number, which he dialed. In a second, her cell phone rang. Alexandra added Nathan's number to her contacts and then put her phone into her purse. "I'll call you tomorrow, if that's okay?"

"That's fine." He stood, placed his hat on his head, nodded, then strode away.

Heart racing, Alexandra watched him make his exit. She had the strange sensation that the date with Nathan Montgomery wasn't going to be as forgettable as she'd thought.

And neither was he.

## Chapter Three

Alexandra stepped into her aunt's house, slipped off her shoes, and placed them on the mat beside the door. After exchanging numbers with Nathan, she'd hugged Kristy and Marissa goodbye. Veronica had still been talking to the man Alexandra had seen her with earlier, and she hadn't wanted to disturb them.

"How was the auction?" Aunt Rose asked, glancing up from her rapidly moving crochet hook. Before Alexandra could answer, Aunt Rose turned to Crystal, Alexandra's teenage babysitter, who was crocheting too, although without the same speed or skill. "You're doing a good job."

Crystal smiled. "Do you think I'll be finished by my dad's birthday? It's in four weeks."

"Yes. And he's going to love that scarf." Turning back to her niece, she repeated, "Well, how was the auction?" without missing a stitch, as if she hadn't been the one to interrupt the conversation.

"It was fun," Alexandra said.

"Did you bid on anyone?"

"Yes."

"Good girl. And did you win?"

"Yes."

"Is this the bachelor auction for the library funds?" Crystal said, putting down her crocheting. "I told my dad to enter, but he just laughed and shook his head. He's never going to find a girlfriend if he doesn't try."

Alexandra didn't know what to make of that comment, so she ignored it and answered Crystal's question. "It was the bachelor auction. And speaking of your father, I should get you home. Just let me check on Chloe."

"She was very good," Crystal said, suddenly all business. She set down her crocheting and picked up a piece of paper from the coffee table. Although Alexandra had told her it wasn't necessary, Crystal insisted on writing detailed notes of everything Chloe did. "She finished her dinner right after you left. We played for a while. She had a bottle at eight thirty and was asleep by nine."

"Thank you. I know that she was in very good hands." Alexandra went to Chloe's bedroom and looked at her sleeping daughter. Her little girl was growing up so fast. Chloe had kicked off the blanket and Alexandra straightened it. Her heart overflowed with love as she caressed her daughter's face.

Chloe stirred and Alexandra reluctantly pulled her hand away.

Being a single mother wasn't easy, and it certainly hadn't been her plan, but Chloe was worth it. Owen was missing out on everything. Not that he cared. He was perfectly happy living his life as a bachelor, seemingly interested in making the world a better place, all the while ignoring his flesh and blood.

Alexandra had met Owen at a fundraiser for childhood cancer research. He'd been so charming. So concerned about the sick children and their worried parents. So sensitive. What a joke. He'd burned rubber in his haste to get away when Alexandra had told him she was pregnant. His family was wealthy and connected—his mother was on the board at the hospital where Alexandra worked. His family wanted her to go away quietly and tried to use their influence to get her fired.

But Alexandra hadn't been without resources of her own. Her mother, Clarice, was the chief of thoracic surgery at that same hospital, and the administration hadn't wanted to risk losing her. Not only that, Alexandra's father was a renowned attorney who'd won hundreds of millions of dollars for his clients. No one in their right mind wanted to go up against Lemuel Jamison in court. If Alexandra had wanted to fight with Owen, she would have won. But she hadn't wanted to battle with him. She'd just wanted to be done with him forever.

In exchange for Owen relinquishing his parental rights, Alexandra had agreed not to seek child support. Of course, Alexandra's father had insisted that Owen create a substantial trust for Chloe. Money couldn't replace a father, but it would guard against financial hardships in the future.

Alexandra closed Chloe's bedroom door, shutting down all thoughts of Owen as well, and then returned to the living room. Crystal had packed up her crocheting and was fastening her jacket. Alexandra grabbed her purse and then took out the agreed upon pay and handed the money to Crystal.

Crystal smiled and shoved the money into her pocket. "Thanks."

"You're welcome."

"I called my dad to let him know you were home. He said that you didn't need to drop me off. He was just leaving the store, so he said he'd pick me up."

Crystal's dad had been a ranch hand, but he'd recently purchased the feedstore in town. "That's nice of him."

The doorbell rang and Alexandra opened the door, letting in Crystal's father.

"How was the auction?" Clay asked.

"Fun. Although I hear you turned down an invitation to enter," Alexandra joked.

Clay grimaced. "That's an invitation I was happy to decline."

"You would have had fun, Dad," Crystal said as she came to stand beside them.

"Your idea of fun is a lot different than mine," Clay said, draping an affectionate arm over Crystal's shoulder and leading her out the door.

"Well, I guess I'll turn in," Alexandra said.

"You don't think you're getting off that easily," Aunt Rose said, patting the pillow next to her. "I want to know everything that happened at the auction. So come sit down and give me all of the details."

"Give me ten minutes to change and I'll tell you everything. Can I get you some tea?"

"No thanks."

Alexandra changed out of her new dress into her pajamas, washed off her makeup, then went back to the front room.

"So, who did you bet on? More importantly, who did you win?"

"Nathan Montgomery."

"Really?" Aunt Rose's eyebrows rose and she laughed. "Of all the men in town, that's the last man I expected you to want to date."

"What makes you say that?"

"Now don't get all huffy. It wasn't a criticism of you or him."

Alexandra blew out a breath. She didn't know why she'd been so touchy. "I know."

"He is a good-looking man, that's for sure. I should have bought a ticket. That way I could have bid on a bachelor or two."

"Really?"

"Sadly there weren't many men in my age group."

"None, to be honest."

"And I don't think those younger men could keep up with me. Of course, I could always teach a young one a thing or two."

Alexandra laughed. "You just might be right."

"Of course I am. So, where are you and Nathan going on your date?"

"We're going to figure it out later."

"That's good. I'm glad that you're starting to get out. You need more than work and Chloe in your life. You need to have fun. A hot fling is just what the doctor ordered."

"It's just one date," Alexandra reminded her aunt, a little appalled—and maybe amused, if she admitted it to herself—at Rose's racy suggestion.

"Well, of course it is, dear. That's how all flings start. On that note, I'm going to hit the hay." Aunt Rose put her crochet hook into her ball of yarn and stood. She gave Alexandra's cheek a gentle pat. "I'll see you in the morning. Good night. Have sweet dreams."

Alexandra was pleased to see that her aunt no longer needed her daily help—if she ever had. When Alexandra first arrived, she'd been surprised to see that her aunt hadn't been as badly hurt as Alexandra had been led to believe. Rose had been getting around—if slowly. Now Alexandra was beginning to suspect that either her aunt had exaggerated the state of her health, or she had conspired with Alexandra's parents to get her out of town after the collapse of her relationship. Either way, coming to Aspen Creek had been a balm to her soul.

Although she loved living with her aunt, Alexandra didn't want to overstay her welcome. After all, Aunt Rose was a senior citizen who'd enjoyed the

peace and quiet of her big, rambling house. She probably longed for the days when she had the house to
herself. Now she had two people living with her. And
one was a baby. Alexandra tried to keep the mess and
noise to a minimum, but that was nearly impossible.

Alexandra had brought up the topic of leaving a
couple of weeks ago, but Aunt Rose had shut down
that conversation. She'd said that Alexandra and Chloe
were welcome to stay for as long as they wanted. Since
Alexandra was still trying to figure out her next move,
and she and Chloe were comfortable here, she had
been glad to hear it.

Once Alexandra was alone, she leaned back in her
chair and closed her eyes. Though she tried not to, she
couldn't stop thinking about Nathan and how handsome he was. Of course, every man in the auction
had been good-looking, but none of the others had
sent shivers racing down her spine from just looking at him. But that didn't mean she had to act on her
attraction. She had no intention of getting involved
with anyone for the foreseeable future. She didn't trust
any man with her heart—or Chloe's—right now. Not
only that, she didn't trust her judgment. So no matter how appealing she found Nathan Montgomery,
he was off-limits.

She would go on their date. And then he would
be out of her life.

Nathan swiped his forearm against his forehead
and leaned against the top rail of the fence. He and his
brothers had just driven the cattle from one grazing

area of the ranch to the other. Most days he enjoyed spending hours on horseback, but today was not one of those days. No matter how he tried, he hadn't been able to get comfortable in the saddle, and he'd been relieved when they'd finally arrived.

He raised his face to the sky. The sun was directly overhead, and he knew that it was only a little bit past noon. Even so, he felt antsy. And he knew why. Alexandra was going to call him today. Knowing that had made it impossible to keep his mind on the task at hand. Twice Miles had spoken to him, and he'd barely heard it. Isaac had finally called him out on his behavior.

It was dangerous to be distracted around animals of this size. The cattle generally stayed with the herd, and there were several trained dogs to keep them in line if they should decide to make a break for it. Even so, Nathan knew he needed to get his head back on straight. Now.

"What's up?" Isaac asked as he and Miles walked over to him.

"Just thinking."

"About that woman who won a date with you at the auction?" Miles asked.

"I can't believe you have the nerve to mention the auction to me," Nathan said, rather than answer.

"You came in third, right behind Marty and the mayor. You raised a lot of money for charity and gained a lot of goodwill for the ranch."

"That's the only reason I'm talking to you today."

Miles laughed and shook his head.

"So are you thinking about her?" Isaac asked.

"Why are you asking me that?" Nathan didn't know why he didn't just answer the question directly. It wasn't a crime to think about her. Alexandra was attractive. Intriguing.

"I'm curious," Isaac said.

Nathan waited for his brother to make a wisecrack and was pleasantly surprised when he didn't. Somehow he forgot that Isaac was actually an adult, capable of having a serious conversation. But the change in his brother's attitude hadn't come with age. Several months ago, Isaac had been named the guardian of a baby girl. To Nathan's surprise, his brother had changed his ways overnight and become a devoted father. Then he'd become involved with Savannah, putting his "love 'em and leave 'em" reputation behind him for good.

"I guess I am thinking about her. She was interesting."

"And sexy."

Nathan raised his eyebrow and gave his brother a hard look.

Isaac laughed and raised his hands in front of him in surrender. "There's no need for you to give me the death stare. I'm just saying she's attractive. That's all. I'm happy with Savannah and not the least bit interested in any other woman. Much less one who has caught your attention. It's about time you found a good woman and settled down."

Nathan laughed. "I know you didn't just say that

to me. Not after you've been out with every woman from here to Denver and back."

"That was before. And now that I've seen the light, I want you to enjoy the same happiness that Miles and I have found."

Miles nodded. Miles and his fiancée, Jillian Adams, had been childhood friends. They'd dated through high school and college before breaking up and marrying other people. As divorced single parents, they had found their way back to each other over the past year, and their connection was stronger than ever.

"I think I'll pass. I have goals that I want to achieve before I even think about getting involved in a serious relationship."

"We know. Your five-year plan," Isaac said, frowning.

Miles rolled his eyes. Nathan already knew his brothers didn't approve of his plan. Luckily, Nathan didn't need their approval.

"Exactly."

"Then why are you standing here daydreaming about Alexandra?"

Before Nathan could think of a suitable reply, his brothers had walked away and mounted their horses.

Isaac looked over at him and called, "Come on. We need to get finished. I want to get back to Savannah and Mia. And you know Jillian will be waiting for Miles. They have wedding plans to finalize."

Nathan shook himself. He was acting like a lovesick teenager instead of a man of thirty. If he was going to run this ranch when his father retired, he needed to keep his head in the game. He couldn't tolerate distractions, no matter how gorgeous the package they came in.

Alexandra was proving to be a distraction he couldn't afford. They'd barely met, and she was already affecting his work. After their date, he was going to have to put her out of his life so he could stay on course. He felt a sharp pain in his chest at that thought. What in the world was that? Why had he felt that pang? It had to be the stress of the day. Or something physical. There was no way his heart would ache at the thought of not seeing a woman he hadn't even known twenty-four hours ago.

He mounted his horse and then got back to work, blocking all thoughts of Alexandra from his mind. It took more effort than it should have, but he managed to stay focused for the remainder of the day.

When he got home, he showered and then looked through the refrigerator for something to heat up for dinner. Two years ago he'd had a five-bedroom house built on the property. He might be single now, but one day he planned to marry and have a family, and they would need a place to live. Building a house now had solved the problem before it had arisen.

Each of his brothers had homes of their own on the ranch too. His parents still lived in the house where Nathan and his brothers had grown up. His mother always cooked plenty of food in case they dropped in for dinner. Nathan ate with his parents on occasion but didn't want to take advantage. Besides, after a hard day at work, he appreciated his solitude.

Antsy and unsettled, he prowled around the kitchen. He knew his nerves were attacking him because he was waiting to hear from Alexandra. He could take control and call her, but he wouldn't. Not because he was afraid it would make him look desperate, although that was a distinct possibility. It was because she had told him she would call. He would trust her to do that at her convenience.

He grabbed a steak out of the refrigerator and seasoned it. Then he stepped onto the patio overlooking his in-ground pool, threw some charcoal on the grill, and lit it. While he waited for the fire to burn down, he lit his firepit, then went back inside, where he threw together a salad and boiled some water for corn. Every once in a while, he picked up his phone to be sure that he hadn't somehow missed Alexandra's call.

They hadn't set up a time for her to reach out. For all he knew, she could be at work. She'd told him that she was a nurse, but he had no idea what her schedule was.

Once the charcoal was perfect, he put the steak on the grill and then sat on a lawn chair in front of the firepit and looked over at the ranch. This was his favorite view of all. There was something about the hills and valleys with the occasional stand of trees that soothed his soul. And no matter which direction he looked, there was nothing to intercept his view. No parking lots. No strip malls. Nothing but nature at its finest.

When the food was ready, he grabbed a cold beer

and then set his dinner on the table. The days were getting shorter and the evenings cooler. Still, there was enough light to see by and the firepit provided sufficient warmth for Nathan to be comfortable while he ate.

As he enjoyed his meal, he let his mind wander. He wasn't the least bit surprised when he found himself thinking about Alexandra. Their conversation last night had been short, but he'd found her to be both intelligent and entertaining. Friendly with a good sense of humor.

She was unmistakably beautiful, but she didn't come across as overly concerned with her looks. She'd been absolutely stunning in her black dress that had clung to her curvaceous body. When she'd walked, he had been mesmerized by the gentle sway of her hips. She was about five-seven, with long, shapely legs that seemed to go on forever.

The phone rang, bringing him back to the present. He immediately looked at the screen. *Alexandra*. He smiled as he answered.

"I hope it's not too late to call," Alexandra said instead of hello. "My daughter didn't feel like going to sleep at bedtime. I had to rock her for a long time tonight."

*Daughter?*

"I didn't know you had a child." He wanted to call back the words a second after they'd burst from his lips. They hadn't come out at all as he'd intended. They'd sounded…bad.

"Yes." She was silent for a moment. "Is that going to be a problem for you?"

He heard the strain in her voice. The barely disguised hurt and disappointment.

"Not at all," he hastened to assure her, uncertain if he was being entirely honest. Odd that she hadn't mentioned her daughter before. But when? And why should she reveal personal details of her life to him? It's not as if they were going to see each other after their date. This wasn't the start of a relationship, so he didn't have to worry about getting attached to her daughter. He didn't have enough time for one person, so he certainly didn't have enough time for two.

"Okay," she said quietly.

He didn't know her well enough to tell if she'd accepted his answer, so he decided to act as if she had and replied to her earlier comment, "It's not too late. Unlike your baby, I don't have to go to bed this early."

"That's good to know."

"How old is your daughter?"

"She's almost one. She's growing so fast every day and I'm just so impressed by how smart she is. How talented. She really is the best little girl in the world." She gave a strangled chuckle. "Sorry. I didn't mean to go on about her. Parental pride run amok, I suppose."

"I didn't mind. I wouldn't have asked about her if I hadn't been truly interested." He loved kids and hoped to have a few of his own one day. But he wasn't anywhere near ready for that role yet. He was just fine playing uncle for the time being to his nieces and nephew.

"Thank you. I was so worried about calling you this late," Alexandra said, then laughed. It was a happy sound that made him smile. "I know you're a rancher. I thought that you guys have to get up early. At least they do in the movies."

"Ah, so I take it that your knowledge of ranching is limited to what you've seen on television."

"And what I read about in books." There was a pause. "But I want to learn more."

"Really? If you want to know more about ranching, ask away. I would be happy to answer any questions you have."

"What kind of ranch do you have?"

"Cattle ranch. It's one of the largest in the state. We breed the best organic beef you'll ever taste in your life."

Although he couldn't see her expression, he felt her smile. The minute that fanciful thought entered his mind, he shoved it aside. That was the kind of idiotic thinking that romantic fools indulged in. No one had ever accused Nathan of being romantic or a fool. In fact, the women he'd dated in the past had accused him of being cold and distant. Uninterested in getting to know them or caring about their hearts. Truth was, he couldn't deny that accusation. Messy emotions could only disrupt his plan. Not that he hadn't tried to be more responsive.

When Janet broke up with him, she'd told him that she'd grown tired of coming in second behind the ranch. He'd been late for dates one too many times or been distracted when they'd been together. Seeing himself through her eyes had been informative and had led to the realization that he wasn't in a position to have a relationship. It would be unfair to a woman for him to pretend otherwise.

"Is that right? Is your beef served in the restaurants in town? If so, I might have eaten it."

"We're in a lot of restaurants in the state, including Aspen Creek." He'd brokered several of those deals and had many more lined up. "If you want, we can go to one of those places for our date. Then you will definitely know that you've enjoyed a Montgomery steak."

"That sounds good. What is a good day for you?"

"How about this Saturday? That is date night."

"So it is." She sounded pleased. He hoped he hadn't given her the wrong idea. He wasn't interested in a relationship. He was simply fulfilling his obligation. Perhaps he should have gone with a Tuesday night. That would have been safer. Well, it was too late to change now. "That sounds like a plan."

The conversation had come to a conclusion, but Nathan was reluctant to end the call. Sadly, he was out of practice with the whole "get to know you" small talk, and the silence between them stretched as he searched for a suitable topic to discuss with her.

Before he could think of something, she spoke. "I suppose I should let you go. I imagine you have to get up early tomorrow."

"I'll call you this week so we can firm up plans for Saturday. Okay?"

"Sounds like a plan."

They said good-night, but Nathan held the phone

for a few long seconds after the conversation ended. Though he told himself to play it cool, one thought echoed through his mind.

He was going to see Alexandra again. And he couldn't wait.

## Chapter Four

"What's up?" Isaac asked, the minute Nathan opened his front door the following Saturday. Ordinarily Nathan was happy to see his brothers, but he didn't have time to shoot the breeze. He was trying to get ready for his date with Alexandra. He'd been looking forward to tonight all week.

"What are you doing here?" Nathan hadn't meant to sound so abrupt, but the words were out there and he couldn't call them back now.

"Just visiting my big brother," Isaac said, pushing away from the doorjamb, stepping around Nathan and into the foyer.

There was a smirk on his brother's face, so Nathan knew he was up to something. Making himself at home, Isaac headed for the kitchen and Nathan followed. Isaac grabbed a beer from the fridge and then leaned against the counter. "Don't you smell nice? Got a date?"

Nathan took the unopened bottle from Isaac's hand and returned it to the refrigerator. "As a matter of fact, I do. What are you doing here? It's Saturday night. Shouldn't you be spending time with your fiancée? Or spoiling my niece?"

"Mom is having a grandmother's night with all of the grandkids. Savannah and the other bridesmaids are taking Jillian out tonight. So I'm on my own."

"And what? You decided to come over here and annoy me?"

"I figured you would be settling in to watch the game. I thought we'd order a pizza and watch it together."

"Well, now you know that I have plans, so you can show yourself out." Nathan walked up the stairs to his bedroom, trying to ignore his brother, who was right on his heels. When he reached his bedroom, he tried to close the door, but Isaac simply stepped inside.

"Come on in," Nathan said sarcastically.

"Don't mind if I do," Isaac said with a laugh. He sat on a chair and crossed his feet at the ankles.

Nathan grabbed his suit from the closet. It was the same one he'd worn to the bachelor auction, with a different shirt to switch it up.

"You aren't wearing that, are you?"

Despite telling himself that his brother was just messing with him, Nathan felt a seed of doubt form in his stomach. "What's wrong with it?"

"Nothing, if you're going to a funeral."

"Are you kidding? A black suit, white shirt, and red tie is classic."

"You'll look like a church deacon. She'll take one look and think you're about to collect the offering."

Despite himself, Nathan laughed.

Uninvited, Isaac stepped into his brother's closet and began to shift hangers aside, shaking his head and mumbling to himself as he discarded one jacket and shirt after the other. "Is this all you have? Work clothes and a bunch of boring suits that look like someone Dad's age would wear?"

"There's nothing wrong with my wardrobe."

"Where are you taking her?"

"We're going to dinner and then, depending on how that goes, maybe dancing at Grady's."

"Then the suit is definitely out. What time are you leaving?"

"Half an hour or so. Why?"

"You're lucky we're the same size. I'm going home and getting you something decent to wear."

"That's not necessary."

Isaac sighed dramatically. "You're going out with Alexandra, aren't you?"

"How did you know?"

"You don't leave this house unless someone—usually me—drags you. Besides, she won a date with you at the bachelor auction. One plus one and all that." Nathan frowned at his brother, who continued, "That is one gorgeous and stylish woman. You want to impress her, don't you?"

"That's a stupid question." Though this was going

to be their only date, he wanted to put his best foot forward and show Alexandra a good time. After all, she had dropped a bucketload of money.

"Then you don't want to show up in the same suit you wore to the auction. You need to wear something else. I'll be back in ten minutes."

"Nothing flashy," Nathan said.

Isaac rolled his eyes. "I wouldn't dream of it."

Nathan shoved the suit back into the closet and shook his head. He couldn't believe he was letting Isaac get inside his mind like this. But aggravating as it was to admit, Isaac had been right about wearing a suit to the auction. That's what the other bachelors had worn. And Nathan had raised the third highest sum. He had known the suit was too formal for Grady's without being told. That's why he'd intended to leave the jacket and tie in the car if they went to the club.

He heard his front door open and a minute later his brother was stepping into the room, several hangers draped over his shoulder. Isaac had brought three shirts, four jackets, and two pairs of pants for Nathan to choose from. As he inspected the coordinating clothes, Nathan had to admit that his brother had chosen well. The clothes were dressy enough to be acceptable at the restaurant and casual enough to wear to the club.

Nathan grabbed a black collarless pullover, a flint gray blazer, and fitted black trousers. After putting them on, he checked his reflection in the full-length mirror. *Not bad*. He glanced over at Isaac, who was lounging on a chair, texting on his phone. "What do you think?"

Isaac looked up and grinned. "Looking good. Much better. You look almost as good as I do in them."

Nathan shook his head. "I would have been fine in my suit too."

"It's pitiful that you actually think that. If you want to change back, you can."

Nathan fastened his watch. "No time."

They walked down the stairs and out of the house. Isaac clapped Nathan's shoulder. "Have a good time tonight."

"I plan on it."

"And if things work out, be sure to give Miles the credit."

"There's nothing to work out. One date. That's it."

"Famous last words," Isaac said with a laugh.

They climbed into their cars and drove away. As Nathan neared Aspen Creek, his excitement grew. He couldn't wait to see Alexandra again. There was something so enticing about the way her thick black hair had skimmed her shoulders every time she shook her head when she'd spoken or laughed. He'd thought about that—and her—more times than he should have this week.

But it was more than her physical attributes that had him pressing the accelerator harder as he sped down the highway. Although they'd only had a couple of conversations, he'd liked what he'd seen of her so far.

Nathan wasn't given to making snap decisions. He knew that people often pretended to be something they weren't. Only after a long time, when they couldn't keep up the act, did the real personality shine through. Even if they didn't have bad intentions, they always tried to put their best foot forward in an effort to make a good first impression. Which was why he'd hadn't allowed himself to get carried away by his reaction to her. She seemed too good. Too perfect. Nobody could be that wonderful.

He looked at his clothes and then laughed out loud. Ironically, he was doing his best to impress Alexandra. He wanted her to enjoy herself tonight. Given what she'd paid, it was the least he could do. But he wasn't going to try to be something that he wasn't. He could try to be as charming as Isaac, but he knew he would never be able to keep it up for long. He was going to be himself and hope for the best. Minus the clothes, which he liked, and which were admittedly better than his. Alexandra was going to see the real Nathan Montgomery. Either she would like him for himself, or she wouldn't.

And really...why did he care that much? He wanted them both to enjoy themselves, but this wasn't the beginning of a relationship. It was their first—and last—date.

He exited the highway, then headed for Alexandra's neighborhood. It was a nice one, but then that could be said of the entire town. There was no poor side of Aspen Creek. There were the affluent and there were the dirty rich. Nathan didn't spend much time in town, but as far as he knew, everyone got on well together.

When he reached Alexandra's aunt's house, he turned off the car and then blew out a deep breath, ridding himself of sudden unexpected tension. He didn't know why he was nervous. It wasn't as if this was his first date in his life. He'd gone out before. Besides, this wasn't a big deal. They weren't going out to discover if there could be something between them. He already knew the answer to that. *No.* There was no room in his life for a woman. This date was simply the fulfillment of an obligation. Once the night was over, he and Alexandra would go their separate ways.

That reminder firmly in his mind, he got out of the car, climbed the stairs of the grand house, and pressed the doorbell. Before the ringing stopped, the door opened. And then Alexandra was standing before him. She was positively stunning. His mouth dropped open. When he realized that he was staring, he closed his mouth and snapped to attention.

"Hello. I hope I'm not too early," he said, even though he knew he was right on time.

"Nope. You've got perfect timing. I just got Chloe to fall asleep. Come on in. I need to get my coat and speak to my babysitter. Then I'll be ready to go."

"Of course." He winced internally at the mention of the babysitter, a reminder that Alexandra was a single mother. After his last relationship, he had developed a hard and fast rule against dating women with children. Even casually. Kids were easy to love. Easy to get attached to. So it was best to avoid them altogether.

Alexandra proceeded him into the front room, and

his eyes followed each step she took. Her red dress fit like a glove, showcasing her sexy body. The fabric stopped in the middle of her well-toned thighs, revealing smooth brown skin that his hands ached to caress. Her matching high heels accentuated her world-class legs. She was dressed perfectly for dinner as well as a few hours at Grady's.

"Hi, Mr. Nathan."

He lifted her eyes from Alexandra's round bottom and smiled at Crystal, the daughter of one of his former ranch hands and current owner of the feedstore. "Hi. How are you?"

"I'm good. I'm babysitting Chloe for Ms. Alexandra. And Mrs. Rose is teaching me how to crochet."

"That's good. We miss seeing you around the ranch. Miles and Isaac said you were the best babysitter they ever had."

"I miss everybody. But now that we live in town, I can't always get out to the ranch to babysit anymore. Will you tell them hi for me?"

"Of course."

Alexandra introduced Nathan to her aunt, who smiled. "It's nice to meet you. You guys have fun. And don't worry about a thing. Crystal has everything under control."

"I know." Alexandra hugged her aunt. "Have a good evening. And either of you can call me if you need to."

"We'll be fine," Crystal said confidently. "I've been babysitting for years."

Nathan and Alexandra exchanged smiles at the

teen's comment. Alexandra picked up her jacket and Nathan immediately took it from her, helping her to put it on. He inhaled and got a whiff of her sweet perfume. It was intoxicating. Once her jacket was on, he stepped away, resisting the temptation to bury his nose in her neck and breathe in her scent.

When they were settled inside his sedan, he turned on the radio to an easy listening station. The sound of the saxophone came over the speaker, and he looked over at Alexandra. "I guess I should have asked before I turned on the radio. What kind of music do you like?"

Alexandra smiled at Nathan's question. She'd been a bundle of nerves all day and his query put her at ease. Though she'd been looking forward to the date all week, dread and worry had been mixed with her excitement. It had been months since she'd been this eager to spend time with a man. Things with Owen definitely had left her wary.

But she didn't feel wary around Nathan. She wasn't worried that he wasn't a good person. Her friends had made it clear that he was. More than that, she was starting to trust her instincts again. They might have led her astray with Owen, but she believed they were right with Nathan. He was honest and trustworthy. He was a good man. The kind of man she could fall for.

That's what had her worried. She didn't want to like him as much as she did; didn't want to be excited about seeing him. She definitely didn't want to open her heart to him. That leap was just too much right now. But his simple question had reminded her that she'd gotten ahead of herself. This was a simple date. A fulfillment of an obligation. She'd been worrying over nothing. "I listen to just about anything."

"No favorites?"

"Not really."

"Come on, everyone likes one type of music more than others."

"My favorites change. It really depends on my mood. Some days are instrumental days. Others are hip-hop. Or classic rock. Or Motown. Of course, in a couple of years my preferences won't matter. I'll be playing the *Bluey* theme song on repeat."

He laughed. "My brothers have kids and I can tell you that will absolutely happen. I confess that I have a couple of kid playlists that the littles—that's what I call my nieces and nephew—make me play whenever they're around."

"*Make* you play?"

"Little kids are monsters."

The idea of a big strong man like Nathan being at the mercy of preschoolers made her laugh. "How old are they?"

"Benji is four. Lilliana is three and Mia is one-and-a-half."

"I have heard about the terrible twos, but I don't believe it can be as bad as all that. It seems like a good nap would get that behavior all sorted."

"If only it was that easy. Of course, your little girl is probably still at that sweet and charming age."

"Yes. She's truly a happy baby. She loves being held and playing with her toys. She's my greatest joy."

"Can she walk?"

"A little. She takes a few steps here and there. But when she's in a hurry to get somewhere, she drops down on all fours. She crawls much faster than she can walk. She had just gone down for the night when you arrived. Otherwise I would have introduced you." She glanced at his strong profile. "Do you have any kids?"

"Me?" He shook his head. "No."

"Do you want any?"

"Maybe one day. I'm definitely not opposed to the idea of being a parent. But I'm not in any hurry either. I'm content to be the favorite uncle for the time being."

That answer was disappointing, but she didn't know why it hurt her heart. It was his truth. And much better than creating a child and shoving it out of his life as Owen had done to Chloe. Besides, she and Nathan were not on their way to starting a relationship. They were simply going on the date that she'd won. Then they were going back to their regularly scheduled lives. She needed to remember that.

"It's a lot easier to be an uncle than a father," Nathan continued. "When they spend time with me, it's only for a few hours at a time. And I always know that I have backup in case I need it. I'm responsible for them for that short period, but when they go home, my responsibility ends. I imagine being a parent is endless worrying."

She huffed out a breath. "I try not to stress too much about every little thing, but I catch myself fretting more than I like to admit. You'd think that being a nurse, I would be more relaxed, but that's not always the case. I still panic about things that are completely out of my control."

"There will be no worrying tonight. We're going to have a good time. A relaxing time."

"That sounds like a plan. Where are we going for dinner?"

"We have reservations at Bliss on Your Lips."

"Really? I'm new to town and even I know reservations there can take up to a month to get and almost twice that long on a Saturday night. How did you get them on such short notice? Did you break a date with someone else?"

He laughed. "You're funny. No. I didn't break a date. I told you, I don't have a girlfriend. And I can't recall the last time I went on a date. My brother is engaged to Jillian Adams. Her brother, Marty, owns the restaurant. Since we're practically family, he found a table for us."

"Party Marty?"

Nathan gave her an odd look. "You know him?"

"No. We've never met. He was in the auction with you, and one of my friends pointed him out."

"He's popular. Hence the name."

"If you go for that type."

"And you don't?" Nathan sounded surprised.

She frowned. "Not even a little bit."

Nathan nodded as if pondering her response. After

a moment, he pulled in front of the restaurant and stopped the car. A uniformed valet ran over. Nathan handed over the keys, pocketed a claim ticket, then helped Alexandra from the car. Nathan held her arm as he led her to the restaurant's entrance, where a uniformed young man greeted them, then opened the door, holding it while they stepped inside.

Alexandra looked around and sucked in a breath. Amazing. She'd known this was a first-class establishment, but even so, she was impressed with the decor. It was exquisite. The luxurious design was as timeless as it was elegant. A two-story chandelier divided the space into an enchanting bar area and an opulent dining room. The tables, draped in pristine white cloths, and lavish blue chairs created the perfect ambience for fine dining.

"This way to your table," the hostess said, pulling Alexandra's attention back to her.

As they walked past the diners, Alexandra inhaled, and her lungs were filled with delicious aromas.

The hostess stopped at a table near large windows that provided an unobstructed view of the mountain peaks.

Nathan held Alexandra's chair and then sat across from her.

"Your server will be here to take your order shortly," the hostess said, handing them each a menu before departing.

Alexandra set her menu on the table and then looked at Nathan. "This place is so chic. It's breathtaking. I absolutely love it." She was gushing, but she couldn't help it.

"I'm glad that you think so. Just so that we're clear, I'm paying for dinner."

"No way. I don't think that's the way it's supposed to go. I won this date with you, so I think I'm supposed to pay." At least that's what she thought. The details had been vague at best.

"That's where you're wrong. You paid for the date. For my company." He winced as he said the words. Clearly he was as uncomfortable with the notion as she'd been at the time. "We're here together. That means that the check is mine."

"That makes sense in a twisted way."

"I'm glad you agree." Nathan picked up his menu. Clearly, in his mind, the case was closed.

"What's good here?" Alexandra asked, glancing at Nathan over the top of hers. He was almost too handsome to look at straight on and foolish butterflies danced in her stomach. She forced herself not to stare. Not that she would be alone in doing that. She'd noticed the way women's heads swiveled as he walked through the restaurant. But no matter how good-looking he was, she wasn't going to let her attraction get out of hand.

Alexandra had no doubt that he had earned his reputation as a hardworking rancher and serious businessman, yet it was easy for her to see that there was more to Nathan Montgomery than that. Beneath that commanding exterior beat the heart of an interesting man. Though she knew it was a bad idea, she really wanted to get to know him on a deeper level.

Lucky for her, Nathan had given no indication that he was interested in more than fulfilling his obligation to go on this date with her. One and done. And since that fit in with her plans, she should be glad. Despite all of his good qualities, he had one glaring flaw. He wasn't interested in becoming a father. He was enjoying his bachelorhood, which was his right. She appreciated his honesty. But she had a child. She and Chloe were a package deal. There was no way she would ever consider becoming involved with a man who wouldn't love her child as his own.

But she needed to get her life back on track before she added another person to the mix. That's what made Nathan perfect for her. They were both clear about what they didn't want. A romance. Or anything that went past tonight. So she was free to let down her hair, so to speak, and just enjoy his company.

"Everything is good," he said, pulling her thoughts back to the present where they belonged. "I generally like the steak. It's Montgomery steak so I can vouch for the quality. They cook it perfectly. It's tender and juicy with just the right amount of smoky flavor. But if you prefer chicken or fish, that will be good too."

"You had me at steak. And since this is Montgomery steak, how can I say no?"

"Good decision. Especially since you're in beef country."

"And having dinner with a Montgomery cattle rancher," she said with a smile.

"That too."

He returned her smile and her heart did a foolish pitter-patter that she tried to ignore.

"Before I moved to Aspen Creek, I didn't think of Colorado as ranch country."

"Most people don't. They think of skiing and other winter sports. And rightly so, since there are some great resorts in the state—including here in Aspen Creek."

"That's exactly what I thought. Probably because I only visited my aunt in the winter. And naturally we went skiing and ice-skating."

"Too bad you never came in the summer. You missed fishing and biking season. And of course hiking."

"I don't get the popularity of hiking. It's just a fancy name for walking outside."

He shook his head and chuckled. She could get used to that sound. "It's more than just walking outside. You're challenging yourself physically, all the while enjoying the beauty of nature."

"Like mountain climbing?"

"Not exactly. But that's also fun. You should try it while you're in town."

"I'll think about it."

"And from the sound of your voice, you've given it all the thought you intend to."

She laughed. "Wise man."

"How long are you going to be in town?"

"That's still up in the air. I'm in the middle of fig-uring out my next move."

"How is that going? If that's not too personal a question."

"Not at all. I'd like an objective opinion."

"I don't know how objective I can be. I happen to think Aspen Creek is the best place in the world to live. I don't understand why people would choose to live anywhere else."

"Part of the charm of Aspen Creek is the small-town feel. That would be lost if too many people lived here."

"True." The waitress came and took their dinner orders, returning within minutes with their drinks and appetizers. By unspoken agreement, they didn't pick up the strands of that conversation until they had tasted everything. It was just as delicious as it looked and smelled.

"So, what factors are you considering," Nathan asked, spearing a seared scallop with his fork.

"Well, first I have to consider my daughter. Chloe is my first priority. She needs to be happy."

"What about her father?"

"Owen isn't in our lives. When I told him that I was pregnant, he let me know in no uncertain terms that he wasn't interested in being a father." Even after all this time, saying the words hurt her. And made her furious. She took a deep breath and then blew it out slowly. "And since I wanted my child to grow up loved, I didn't try to change his mind. We agreed that he would give up his parental rights and I wouldn't sue him for child support."

"He didn't want his child?" Nathan's voice rang with disgust.

"No. And I was not going to try to force him to be in her life. Chloe deserves better than that."

"So do you."

The sincerity in his voice warmed her heart and she smiled. "Thank you."

"Did you come to Aspen Creek looking for a fresh start?"

"Yes and no. I had been trying to figure out my next move when Aunt Rose hurt her hip. When she was released from the hospital, my parents wanted her to move in with them. Aunt Rose wouldn't think of it. She loves her independence. We were all worried about her, and I was thinking of getting a new job, so I asked if I could come and stay with her for a while. She agreed. Since I'm a nurse, I could help care for her."

"That makes sense."

"Yes. But I wasn't here long before I realized that Aunt Rose didn't need all that much help. I sometimes wonder if she didn't exaggerate her injury in order to give me an excuse to move here. A new purpose in life so to speak."

"Would that be so bad?"

"Not really. Because I can tell you that I was devastated by the way things went with Owen," Alexandra said, and then paused. She didn't ordinarily share so much of herself, and never with someone she just met. Yet here she was, opening up to Nathan. It felt right, somehow, so she continued, "Never in a million years would I have thought he'd treat me and Chloe that way. He seemed like such a good guy. Concerned about all the same things that concerned me. Making the world a better place might really be important to him, but he definitely wasn't husband or father material. Too bad I didn't see that in the beginning. I would have saved myself so much needless pain."

"Maybe you didn't see it because he didn't show it to you. The guy probably guessed that if you knew all about him, you wouldn't want him. And he wanted to be with you enough to lie and hope that it would be enough for you."

"Wow. That's very kind of you to say. But Owen doesn't deserve it. I don't think he gave my feelings a second thought. He did what was best for him."

"Then you're definitely better off without him. And so is Chloe."

"Agreed." She took a sip of her wine. It was delicious and deserved to be savored over pleasant conversation, not soured by bitter topics like her failed romance. "Enough about me and my failed relationship. I'll be happy to never mention Owen again."

The waitress appeared with their meals then, and Alexandra inhaled the wonderful aroma of her steak. Nathan must have read her mind because he smiled. "Wait until you taste it."

She picked up her knife and cut a slice. It was tender and juicy. She popped it into her mouth and a moan of pleasure immediately followed. "Oh my goodness. This is good."

"I'm glad you think so. That makes all the days

of hard work at the exclusion of everything else—including a social life—worth it. Being single-minded has paid off."

"I don't believe that for a moment. There's more to you than just being a cattle rancher. You've already shown that much."

His eyebrows lifted as if he were trying to figure out when and how he'd given himself away. "Have I?"

"Yes. Consider the way we met. That was a charity auction. You didn't have to participate, but you did. To be honest, I don't think I would have had the nerve."

"Let me tell you a little secret," he said, a mischievous smile on his face. "If I could have thought of a way to get out of it without damaging the ranch's reputation and simply made a cash donation instead, I would have done it in a heartbeat. But nothing came to mind."

She laughed. "You should have tried harder. I could have come up with an excuse on a moment's notice. My car ran out of gas. The dry cleaner ruined my dress. The moon is too full. Anything."

He laughed. "*The moon is too full?* Where were you when I needed you? You weren't around, so I was stuck standing up on the stage while my mom's walking buddy bid on me." He shuddered.

"Which just shows what a good sport you are."

"Maybe." He leaned back in his chair. The look that he gave her made her heart flutter. "But I like the way things worked out."

## Chapter Five

Nathan couldn't believe he'd just blurted out that comment. Especially since he was determined not to lead Alexandra to believe he wanted more than this one date. This was why he focused on business and left the wining and dining to Isaac. He supposed he could play the game, but that wasn't his style. Being honest had served him well in business. It would do no less in his personal life. He'd always been clear with women that he wasn't interested in anything serious right now. Business came first. And it would for the foreseeable future.

"I'm pretty pleased with everything myself," Alexandra said. Her smile was warm and he felt his body heat rising. Still, he reminded himself yet again that there was no room in his life for a woman. Even one as appealing as Alexandra. But then, since she wasn't looking for anything either, there was no danger that she would expect a commitment from him.

He swallowed more wine, taking the opportunity to sneak a peek at her. When she glanced up and caught him staring, her cheeks took on an attractive pink tinge.

"Well, the night is young. There's plenty of time for us to spend together and get to know each other better. That is the best way, you know."

Wait, why did he just say *that*? That almost sounded like he wanted her to be in his life for more than tonight. Something he'd already decided was definitely *not* going to happen.

"True. You really are wise to be so young."

"It comes from being the oldest child."

"As the youngest child, I'll have to take your word for it." She batted her long lashes at him. "Of course, we can talk while we eat. I can get to know more about you over dessert."

He nodded. When she looked at him like that, he would tell her anything she wanted to know. "Absolutely. You've probably already guessed that I love living in Colorado. There is something good to do every season, and I try to do it. Although I like being a rancher, I like the business side more. There's something about looking for new opportunities and then finding them that I find so fulfilling. Finding new markets for our beef. Negotiating contracts. I enjoy it all. Of course, I'm not a big fan of schmoozing clients, but it goes with the territory."

"Really? I'd take a dinner I didn't have to cook any

day of the week. Especially if it's this good. Where do I sign up for schmoozing?"

She flashed him a smile that made his heart skip a beat.

Ordering himself to calm down, he focused on their conversation. "I take it there's not much wining and dining in nursing."

"Not even a little bit. But there are other advantages. I like interacting with the patients, doing what I can to help them to feel better. Sometimes an encouraging word mixed with the right amount of medicine is all it takes to brighten a patient's day."

"What made you decide on nursing?" Despite telling himself to stick to generic, impersonal topics, he wanted to know what made her tick. He'd already decided that she was off-limits, so what was the harm in learning more about her?

"Medicine was one of the two career options in my family."

"I hope you're kidding."

She shrugged. "In a way. My mother is a doctor. She's a thoracic surgeon. Chief of her department. My father is a lawyer. Those are the careers that I saw at home. I know people joke about joining the family business, but it often happens. Children follow in their parents' footsteps." She gestured at him and he nodded.

"I see your point."

"My brother, Joshua, is a doctor, and my sister, Victoria is a lawyer. I liked medicine, but I didn't want to be a doctor. Not that there is anything wrong with that. I just felt like nursing was more for me."

"And are all of you happy with your career choices?"

"We are." She took a bite of her steak and then pointed her fork at him. "And we've done it again. We're talking about me. Tell me about your childhood. Something unexpected. Something that is completely out of character for you."

"Hmm." He thought for a minute She'd told him bits about herself, so it was only fair to share. But he didn't want to talk about being rejected by former lovers. He needed to keep the mood light. "My brothers and I had a singing group."

Her eyes widened and then she laughed. The sweet sound made his heart race and he ordered himself not to react that way again. "Really. What kind of music did you guys sing?"

"Oh. A little of this and a little of that. Ballads. Dance music. Boy band. Whatever was popular."

"How old were you?"

"Young. Junior high school age."

"Did you guys play instruments?"

"No. Our friends played for us. We were sure we were going to be big stars. You know, sold-out concerts in stadiums full of screaming fans. Grammy awards. The whole nine yards."

"I get the picture." She tilted her head. "Who was the lead singer?"

"I was. But in all honesty, Miles should have been. He's the best singer in the family by far."

"So why were you the lead singer?"

Nathan shrugged. "I was the oldest."

"And age has its privilege?" One corner of her mouth lifted in a half smile that made the blood race through his veins.

"That's the way I saw it at the time. It wasn't easy, knowing that my younger brother had more talent than I did. I figured that since I was older, I should have been better. I could rope and ride better than Miles and Isaac, so to me, it logically followed that I should be able to do everything better. Including sing. Of course, I couldn't."

"That had to be a hard lesson to learn."

"Trust me, it was a shock to my system. I liked being better at everything than they were. I didn't understand that learned skills were different from innate talent. I didn't learn it back then. Truth be told, I'm still learning it."

She grinned. "Growing up stinks, doesn't it?"

"Yes. Nobody likes being a reasonable adult."

"So where did you guys perform?"

He leaned back in his chair, as he thought back to those days. "School talent contests. We actually did well in a couple of them. We came in second in one and third in the other. Once we performed at a birthday party."

"Oh. The big time."

The mischief in her voice made him realize just how much fun he could have with her and alarm bells began ringing inside his brain. He ignored them.

"You'd better know it. For about a week I walked

around like a big shot. I just knew we were on our way." He laughed.

"Your one brush with fame." She giggled. "Then what happened?"

"Nothing. The gigs dried up. And practicing wasn't nearly as much fun as performing. One big fight and it was all over. Still, it was fun while it lasted."

She gave him an admiring smile. "You sang in a band. That is something I would have never guessed about you."

"Your turn," he said.

"To?"

"Reveal something unexpected about yourself."

Her brow wrinkled as she appeared deep in thought and that expression was sexier than it should have been. "Well, I can safely say that I have never been in a singing group. You and your brothers might be good singers, but I can honestly say I have no musical talent at all. Okay, that's not completely accurate. I can't sing but I took piano lessons as a girl."

"Did you like it?"

"Not as much as Joshua did. He's excellent. He could play professionally if he wanted to. I was nowhere near as good. After five years of private lessons, I finally convinced my parents to let me quit. In a pinch, I might be able to play 'Für Elise' and a little bit of 'Moonlight Sonata.'"

"That's it?"

"Yes. I did a lot better in my dancing lessons."

"What kind of dance?"

"Oh, you know, the usual. Ballet and tap when I

was in grammar school. In high school I added jazz and modern, which I preferred. Lucky for me, those lessons stuck. I'm a great dancer."

"She said modestly," Nathan said with a grin.

"If I'm going to be brutally honest about my flaws, I'm going to be just as honest about my skills."

"I like the way you think."

She winked. "It works for me."

"If you're up to it, I'd like to take you dancing. That way you can let me see your moves."

"I am totally up for dancing. Just say the word and I'm ready." She lifted the fork with the last bit of her steak to her mouth and shimmied in her chair. The innocent move was enticing. He couldn't wait to see her body move in time to the music on the dance floor. Not only that, but at some point the DJ was likely to play a slow song and Nathan might get the chance to hold Alexandra in his arms.

"Would you like anything else? Dessert?"

"No. Everything was delicious, but I don't have room for another bite."

"Then let's get going."

He paid the check, including a tip, then escorted Alexandra from the restaurant. Once they were in the car, he turned to her. She was staring at him, a smile on her face. Her sweet expression did things to his insides that he had difficulty ignoring.

"I can't remember the last time I went dancing," he confessed.

"It's been a while for me too."

"I'm taking you to Grady's. It's the most popular club in Aspen Creek. It's the best kept secret in town."

"I've never been there. I was supposed to go with my friends one night, but Chloe got sick, so I had to cancel."

"They have a great house band—Downhill From Here—and one of the best DJs around. Occasionally they have a guest band, but I don't know if one will be there tonight."

"And the crowd?"

"Everyone is friendly. It's a mature crowd—everyone is there to have a good time."

"Sounds like fun."

"It is. We'll be there in a few minutes. I hope you have on your dancing shoes."

She held up a foot and he took another opportunity to check out her calf. It was shapely and sexy as hell. Her shoes had four-inch heels, but he'd seen women dancing in higher. He didn't know if their feet hurt, but he'd never heard one of them complain.

He parked, helped her from the car, and they went inside Grady's. Up-tempo music played. It was loud, but not too loud for conversation. The room was enormous, and the border of the room was lined with black and silver booths.

Nathan led her through the room and they found a booth near the dance floor with a view of the stage. A DJ was spinning records and several people were already on the floor. Alexandra and Nathan dropped their jackets onto their seats.

Nathan smiled at her. "Do you want to dance, or would you rather watch for a while?"

Instead of speaking, she shook her shoulders and wiggled her hips in a move that sent his mind down a road it had no business traveling. And yet, he couldn't stop imagining Alexandra in his arms. In his bed. He forced the image away. No matter how enticing she was, they weren't going to be spending any time in his bed. Or hers.

"You don't even need to ask."

He took her hand and led her to the dance floor. Her skin was warm and soft, and her hand fit perfectly in his. Electricity shot from his fingers and throughout his body. He knew he should release her hand, but what was the fun in that? He didn't feel like being responsible right now. Besides, no harm could come from just holding hands.

She spun around and his eyes instantly shot to her sexy bottom. Hypnotized, he was frozen in place.

She turned around and stared at him. She stopped moving and frowned. "Please don't tell me you can't dance."

"Oh, I can dance," he said, beginning to move. He did a few fancy steps and then looked at her.

She smiled and nodded, then began to dance again. "Oh yeah. You have the moves. I think you'll be able to keep up with me."

They danced together as if they'd been partners for years. As one song merged into the next, it became clear that Alexandra had been blessed with natural grace. Her moves were easy and flowed in time to the music. She also possessed an innate sexiness that was making him sweat. He wasn't looking for romance or even a one-night stand. Those things always ended in disaster, hurt feelings, and disappointment. Yet that knowledge couldn't make his body behave in the way that he wanted.

"Why are you frowning?" Alexandra asked as she shimmied up to him and brushed her hand against his chest, a teasing smile on her face. "Don't tell me that you're counting the steps in your head."

Laughing, he reached out and grabbed her waist, holding her in place. The motion from her hips as she moved to the music was nearly his undoing, and he had to force himself to concentrate on what he'd been about to say. "Cute. I don't need to count."

The up-tempo music faded into a slow song, and she draped her arms across his shoulders, looping them around his neck. He slid his arms around her waist as if holding her pressed against him was the most natural thing in the world, and they swayed together to the ballad. He closed his eyes and savored the moment as the saxophone slid into a sultry solo. Although he'd danced with many women in his life, he'd never felt anything quite this satisfying.

As they danced, Nathan was struck by just how well they fit together. Not just physically, although their bodies fit together like two puzzle pieces. It was the *way* they moved. It was as if she sensed where and how he was going to move before he did. And he was just as able to anticipate her next move. They were completely in sync. She moved closer and her sweet scent wrapped around him, inflaming his desire even more.

"This is nice," she said and sighed. "I could get used to this."

Alexandra wanted to call back the words the instant they'd fallen from her mouth. She couldn't believe that she'd thought them, much less said them out loud. But from the way Nathan jerked, she knew that he'd heard her.

She stepped back, creating the physical distance she needed. Luckily the song ended right then, so her movement looked natural. The DJ announced that the house band would be playing soon and everyone began to vacate the dance floor.

Although the light was dim, Alexandra could still see the expression on Nathan's face. He looked as stunned as she felt. She needed to get a hold of her emotions and her mouth before things got out of hand. She and Nathan were perfect for each other because neither of them was looking for a relationship. This date was a onetime thing never to be repeated. Yet somehow, dancing close to him and being held in his strong arms, she'd lost track of that important fact.

Nathan was turning out to be totally different than she'd expected him to be. He was charming. Funny. He'd gone out of his way to put her at ease. His personality and great body made him the total package.

But she hadn't anticipated just how good she would feel in his arms. How heavenly moving together to the music would be. Being held in his embrace, even just while dancing, had revealed that his muscles were just as hard as they looked. His years of physical labor had definitely paid benefits.

And he smelled so good. When she'd been in his arms, she'd gotten a whiff of his masculine scent. It was more than his cologne that appealed to her. It was his own natural scent that had teased her all night. Tempting her to forget her vow to keep him at a distance.

Even though she was in danger of crossing the line, she didn't want the night to end yet. "I guess we should sit down so we can watch the band."

Nathan nodded and she breathed a sigh of relief. She hadn't ruined everything. The date would go on.

"Would you like something to drink?" Nathan asked.

"I would love a soft drink," she replied. Hopefully it would cool her off.

"I'll be right back," he said and then headed for the bar. He was back shortly with their drinks.

Alexandra and Nathan didn't talk much as the band played. They were just as good as Nathan promised, and when their set was over, Alexandra and Nathan rose to their feet and applauded with the rest of the crowd.

"That was great," Alexandra said.

"They always put on a good show."

The conversation lagged. Clearly her words from earlier in the evening still lingered in the air, casting a pall over the evening. She decided to take the reins of the conversation since she was the one who'd caused the unease between them. "About what I said earlier…"

"Forget about it."

"I will. But first I want to repeat that I'm not looking for a relationship. I don't have room in my life for a man. Nor am I interested in one."

"Same here."

"Actually, I don't think I'll ever be ready to put my heart on the line in a relationship."

Something that looked like disappointment mingled with sorrow flitted across his face before vanishing. "Don't say that. You never know what will happen in the future. You might meet someone. You should keep your options open."

"I don't see you running to get involved with anyone."

"Not right now. But I'm not against the idea. I want to get married in a few years, after I have accomplished my goals with the ranch. Right now, I'm not in the position to have a relationship. I don't have time to give a woman the attention she deserves. I tried a few times before and it always ended in disappointment. And pain. I'm not willing to take that risk when I know I'm not in a place to be a full partner. I'm not selfish enough to do that."

"That's exactly why I'm not interested in a man. Not because I have a ranch to run, but because I know that I don't have anything to offer a man. My heart wouldn't be in it. Nobody deserves to be disappointed and hurt. Especially when it can be avoided."

"Then we're in agreement."

"Totally," Alexandra said, although being around Nathan made her wish things could be different. But they couldn't so she forced down her longing and dis-appointment. "And on that note, I suppose we should get going. It's getting late, and I have to drive my babysitter home."

"Crystal is a nice girl. Her father used to work on our ranch, and she used to babysit for Miles and Isaac."

"Chloe loves her. So does Aunt Rose. I told Crystal that if we get home late, she could go to sleep if she wants, since Aunt Rose is there."

Nathan laughed. "How did that go over?"

"Poorly. She told me that she was a professional and would be staying up."

They put on their jackets and then moved through the crowd. When they were outside, Alexandra glanced up at the sky. The moon and stars were shining in the deep blue expanse. It was just so beautiful that it took her breath away. She'd lived in Aspen Creek for months, but she was still struck by its beauty.

The night had grown chillier while they were in-side, and she shivered.

"Cold?" Nathan asked.

"A little." She tightened her jacket around her, shoved her hands into her pockets, and moved closer to him.

"Then let's get moving," Nathan said, wrapping his arm around her shoulder. The heat from his body en-circled her, warming her. Despite telling herself that the attraction should be ignored, his nearness made the fire inside her grow hotter and she leaned closer.

Once they were inside the car, Nathan turned on the heat. Alexandra leaned back and allowed herself to reflect on the night. It had been wonderful, and she hated to see it end.

When they reached her house, Nathan parked. "I'll get your door for you."

"Thank you."

As Nathan rounded the front of the car, Alexandra couldn't help but smile. It was so nice to have someone spoil her. Nathan Montgomery was proof that chivalry wasn't dead.

When her door opened, she took his hand and allowed him to help her from the car. As they climbed the stairs to the house, her heart began to pound with anticipation. This hadn't been a traditional date—she'd paid for his time—but even so, she wondered how it was going to end.

Would they simply say good-night before he walked down the stairs, and she went into the house? That seemed a bit bland. Cold even. Not a fitting end to the great date they'd had. Or would they shake hands? That seemed too businesslike even for a serious businessman like Nathan.

Or, would they kiss? On the cheek? Or on the lips? Her heart skipped a beat at the thought. She ordered herself to stop this ridiculous line of thinking. She'd never put this much thought into the end of a date before. But then, she'd never been in this position before either. Never been as attracted to a man before. Never wanted to kiss a man this badly.

Never been so sure that kissing Nathan was the wrong thing to do.

Alexandra had forgotten to turn on the porch light,

so the moon and stars provided the only illumination. As a result, she and Nathan were standing in the shadows. It felt intimate. Cozy.

She turned to look at him, only to find him staring at her. They gazed into each other's eyes for a brief moment. Neither of them spoke, but in that moment they didn't need words to communicate. His eyes grew dark with intensity. Then he reached out and brushed a strand of hair behind her ear, then caressed her cheek.

She placed her hand on Nathan's chest. His heart was pounding, beating in time with hers.

One corner of his lips lifted in a sexy half smile. "Alexandra, I really want to kiss you now."

Her breath caught. "So, what's stopping you?"

Slowly, as if giving her a chance to reconsider, Nathan lowered his head. Anticipation built inside her, and by the time his lips brushed against hers, she was burning with desire. Her knees weakened and she grabbed on to his shirt. Electricity spread throughout her body, leaving a tingling sensation in its wake.

Nathan wrapped his arms around her waist, and she moved closer, molding her body against his. She opened her mouth to him, and his tongue swept inside, deepening the kiss. Their tongues danced and tangled, and she savored the taste of him. She moaned and tried to get even closer to him.

Gradually she became aware that Nathan was slowly easing back, ending the kiss. Resisting the urge to cling to him, she struggled to regain control of her ragged breathing. Even though the kiss was over, aftershocks reverberated throughout her, prolonging the pleasure. Alexandra tried to talk, but she couldn't manage to gather enough words to form a coherent thought.

"Wow," Nathan said. "That was totally unexpected."

"Yeah." Alexandra shook her head in a futile attempt to clear it.

"And it shouldn't have happened," Nathan said. That statement was as good as cold water in the face. Her mind was clear now.

"I know." She had regained enough strength to stand without his assistance, so she stepped away from him. "Let's just consider that a temporary loss of control."

"A momentary lapse in judgment," he said. His voice was low. Gritty.

"And one that won't be repeated."

"It can't be repeated."

She nodded. "Agreed."

He edged away from her. "I need to get going."

"And I need to take Crystal home."

He started down the stairs, hesitated, then turned back to her. "It's been great getting to know you, Alexandra. Maybe I'll see you around."

"Yeah. Same."

Alexandra watched until he had driven away before she stepped inside the house and closed the door. Though she'd only just met Nathan, a feeling of loneliness swept over her and she longed to call him back. But she couldn't. Their date was over.

And he was out of her life.

## Chapter Six

"How was your date last night?" Michelle Montgomery asked Nathan the following day. Even though they all lived on the same ranch and saw each other during the week, Nathan's mother cooked a big dinner every other Sunday, so the family could spend quality time together.

Even though Miles and Isaac were engaged, and building their lives with their respective fiancées, they still took the time to join the family for dinners. Just not as early, as they had children to wrangle—which was why, on this Sunday, Nate found himself alone with his parents.

"How did you hear about that?" Nathan asked. He and his mother were setting the dining room table. He had placed the embroidered cloth that they'd used for every Sunday dinner for as long as he could remember onto the big dining room table, and his mother was smoothing out wrinkles.

"Was it supposed to be a secret?" Pausing, she glanced up.

"No. I guess it wasn't."

"Then did you have a good time?"

He nodded, and despite wanting to play it cool, he couldn't suppress his smile as he recalled the night. "Alexandra is very nice. We had dinner and then went to Grady's."

"I don't think I know her."

"She hasn't lived in town long. Alexandra is a pediatric nurse. She and her daughter are staying with her great-aunt, Rose Kenzie, for a while."

Michelle set a fork on a napkin and then looked at him. "You seem to know quite a bit about her."

"We had to talk about something."

"That's true. After all, she did spend a pretty penny on you." Michelle's eyes sparkled with mirth.

"Exactly."

"I still can't believe you participated in the auction. Isaac, yes. That's right up his alley. You? Not so much. I'm glad you stepped out of your comfort zone."

"You know I'll do anything for the ranch. Goodwill goes a long way."

Michelle frowned, something she rarely did and pointed a fork in his direction. "There's more to life than this ranch, you know."

"I know. But the ranch is important."

"Like finding a nice girl," Michelle said as if he hadn't replied. This was her favorite topic of discussion. Before his brothers had become involved, her focus had been split among the three of them. As the last man standing, Nathan got her undivided attention.

"There's time for that," he said as always. Not that it mattered. Michelle would not be deterred.

"Now that your brothers are settling down, you should take a page from their books."

Nathan inhaled and slowly blew out the breath. "You and Dad always told us to follow our own paths. That's what I'm doing."

"Did someone mention me?" his father said, coming into the dining room, a stack of plates in his hands. Edward was in his late fifties, but his posture was as erect as ever. He was just as strong as he'd always been. There was no man Nathan admired more than his father.

"I was just reminding Mom that the two of you raised us not to follow the crowd."

"That's right. A man has to blaze his own path."

"There's nothing that says he has to walk that path alone," Michelle countered, laying the last fork on a napkin with extra emphasis.

Edward laughed. "I take it that you've decided to make a match for Nathan now."

"Now that Isaac and Miles are part of a couple, she's turned her sights on me," Nathan said mournfully.

"You have to admit that your brothers are with wonderful women."

"They are."

"You had better get out there before all of the good women are gone," Michelle said.

"Michelle," Edward said softly. "Leave the boy alone. He'll find someone when it's time."

"Thank you," Nathan said.

"Besides, you know how stubborn he is. The more you push him, the harder he'll pull in the opposite direction."

"Hey!" Nathan objected.

"Eventually he'll realize that you're right," Edward said.

Nathan frowned. "Just whose side are you on?"

"Nobody's. I don't take sides, you know that."

"Who's pushing?" Michelle said innocently. "All I did was ask him about his date last night."

"Oh yes. The date with that woman from the auction," Edward said. "I imagine it must have been pretty awful."

"What makes you say that?" Nathan asked.

"She had to pay a man to go out with her. Only a desperate woman would do that. So, what was wrong with her? Was she rude? Boring?"

"Alexandra was none of those things," Nathan said. "She is kind, smart, and very interesting. She bid on me as a way to support charities."

"So, there was nothing wrong with her?" Edward set a plate beside the silverware and glanced at Nathan, a skeptical expression on his face.

"No. She was perfect."

His father flashed a *gotcha* smile. "Is that right?"

Nathan narrowed his eyes. "This was a setup. The

two of you are working together to get me to settle down."

"Proof of how well two people can work together," Edward said. He put an arm around Michelle's shoulder, pulled her close, then kissed her cheek.

"So, how was the date?" Michelle asked.

"It was fine. But it's not going to be the start of a relationship if that's what you're asking."

"Why are you so certain?" Michelle asked.

"Especially if you think she's perfect," his father said with a grin.

"Because we talked about it. Neither of us is interested in a relationship. She's might not even stay in Aspen Creek." Just saying the words caused an ache in Nathan's chest, but he ignored it.

"Hmm," Michelle said. "I didn't know that."

"Now you do. So can you please drop it?"

"If that's what you want," Michelle said. "I was just making conversation."

"It is." Nathan grabbed the glasses from the cabinet and then placed them beside the plates.

"Did I mention that Carol's daughter is moving back to Aspen Creek? She could use a friend."

"Mom," Nathan said. "I'm fine on my own."

"Really? Then why are you so grumpy?" Michelle asked.

"Hey, we're here," Miles called from the entry, the door slamming closed behind him.

"Thank goodness," Nathan muttered to his parents' obvious amusement.

A minute later, Benji raced into the room, his sister, Lilliana, hot on his heels. Jillian followed more slowly, a cake carrier in her hands.

"Hi, Uncle Nathan," Benji said, wrapping his arms around Nathan's leg.

"Hi, Uncle Nathan," Lilliana echoed, grabbing his other knee and holding on.

"Hey, it's the littles," Nathan said. He leaned down and scooped them up, holding them in his arms. "Have you been good?"

They nodded, managing to look as innocent as angels. Nathan wasn't fooled for a moment. He babysat them from time to time. He'd been caught off guard the first time, but now he knew the havoc they could wreak when they were together. After spending a few hours alone with them, he was always as exhausted as he'd be after putting in a full day of work.

He set them on their feet. "Go say hi to Grandma and Grandpa."

Nathan walked over to Miles and Jillian, who were smiling at each other. Their wedding, two weeks away, was a long time coming. Although they'd broken up with each other years ago and subsequently had disastrous marriages, it had always been clear that they belonged together. Nathan was happy that they'd found each other again and wished them a lifetime of happiness.

But married life was for them. Not him. An image of Alexandra's face flashed before him, but he set it aside.

A relationship was not in the cards for him right now. Especially not with a single mom.

"What's going on?" Miles asked.

"Nothing really," Nathan replied to his brother before kissing Jillian on her cheek. "Excited about the wedding?"

"Only two weeks to go," Jillian said gleefully. "Then we'll be a family officially."

"As far as I'm concerned, you've always been a part of this family. But I'm glad you guys are making it official."

"Best decision I made in my life," Miles said.

"Darn right," Jillian said. "And don't you forget it."

"Never." Miles's voice was serious. A vow. The look he and Jillian shared was so intimate Nathan felt as if he was intruding on a private moment.

He was about to excuse himself when Jillian spoke. "I'm going to help get food on the table."

Once they were alone, Nathan turned to his brother. "Nervous?"

"Not even a little bit. I'm marrying the love of my life."

"I know the four of you will be so happy together."

Miles was nodding when the front door opened. Isaac and Savannah stepped inside, each holding one of Mia's hands.

Edward stepped into the room. "Well, look who finally got here. It's Grandpa's baby girl."

"Pa-pa," Mia exclaimed. She pulled her hands free and ran across the room as fast as her little legs could take her. When she reached Edward, he bent over and scooped her into his arms and planted a kiss on her cheek. Laughing, she kissed him back. Edward tossed her into the air, and she laughed again.

"I'm about to put dinner onto the table, so go wash your hands," Michelle said, coming into the room. She reached out her arms for Mia, who shook her head and then leaned against Edward's chest. "All right, little one. I know how you love your Pa-pa. I'm partial to him too, so I can't blame you for having good taste."

"Do you need help?" Savannah asked.

"I could always use another pair of hands," Michelle said, looping arms with Savannah and returning to the kitchen.

"You know your mother is thrilled to finally have daughters," Edward said, before carrying Mia out of the room to find the other kids.

"Yeah, and she's looking for me to add a third," Nathan said.

"So, are you going to step up, big brother?" Isaac asked. "Or are you going to break Mom's heart?"

"Don't start," Nathan said, shoving his brother's shoulder. "I already had the conversation with her and cleared the air. She understands that I'm not going to be bringing a woman into the family."

"You don't actually believe that's the end of it," Miles said.

"Of course I do." As much as he could. He knew that his mother would try to stay out of his love life, but that eventually she would revert back to her old ways. She couldn't help herself. She was a romantic at heart. She was happily married and believed everyone would be happier if they were part of a matched set. Like socks.

His brothers exchanged glances and then looked back at him. Isaac smirked. "No, you don't."

"You're right. I'm just hoping for a reprieve. With the wedding coming up, she should be distracted for a while."

"The wedding is practically here. Once that's over, she'll be turning her attention back to you," Miles said.

"Not if Isaac and Savannah start planning their wedding," Nathan said, turning to his youngest brother.

Isaac laughed and shook his head. "Sorry, we won't be able to save you. We will be getting married, but we aren't ready to set a date. We want to take things slowly. Given Savannah's past, that's understandable."

Savannah had been married before she'd met Isaac. Her husband and four-year-old son had been killed by a drunk driver. She'd moved to a cabin bordering the Montgomery ranch in an effort to escape the pain. She and Isaac had met and quickly fallen in love.

"How slowly?"

"We're thinking about late next summer. Or maybe early next fall."

"Really? That's great," Nathan said. "You guys deserve all the happiness in the world."

"Thanks."

"Dinner is on the table," Michelle called from the dining room. "Are you going to stand around talking, or are you coming to eat?"

"Eat," they chorused.

Michelle was a big believer that the children should be included at the table with the adults, and Benji and Lilliana were sitting on booster seats and Mia's high chair was scooted up to the table. After saying the blessing, Michelle began to serve the roasted chicken, baked macaroni and cheese, green beans, and rolls.

Dinner was a lively affair with plenty of conversation and laughter. After dessert had been eaten, Nathan and his brothers cleared the table, put away the leftovers, and cleaned the kitchen. Everyone hung around for a while longer, relaxing and talking while the kids played. When Nathan headed home, his stomach was full, yet he felt oddly empty.

Being around his brothers and their fiancées made him long for more in his life than work. Not a romance. His mind remained unchanged about that. But after his date with Alexandra, he appreciated the value a woman's presence could bring to his life. Spending time with her had been more pleasurable than the solitude he usually enjoyed. And she was certainly a lot more fun than his brothers. A little female companionship every now and then wouldn't hurt. A woman who could be his friend. Just a friend.

Too bad she wasn't interested.

Alexandra laughed as she wiped smeared spaghetti sauce from Chloe's face.

Echoing her, Chloe laughed and then clapped her hands, clearly pleased with something.

"All done. Time for your bath." Alexandra unstrapped Chloe from her high chair and carried her into the bathroom. Once Chloe was in the warm water, she began to play with her toys. Alexandra sat on the side of the tub, watching as her daughter poured water from one cup to another.

This had been a good day. Aunt Rose had met up with some of her friends for a matinee followed by an early dinner and then a Spades tournament, leaving Alexandra and Chloe on their own. Mother and daughter had spent the day playing with dolls and blocks.

Although Alexandra had enjoyed playing with her daughter, her mind kept drifting to Nathan and their date. No matter how hard she tried, she couldn't stop replaying the highlights of the night. The memories had been complete with the emotions she'd felt, including the ones she'd done her best to suppress.

Everything about dinner had been perfect. The food had been delicious, living up to the restaurant's reputation. Nathan had been so easy to talk to and their conversation had flowed easily. The night would have been a success if the date had ended there.

But it hadn't. They'd gone to Grady's. Dancing with Nathan had been the ultimate pleasure. He definitely had the moves and she'd enjoyed watching him in action. But it was being held in his strong arms as they danced to slow, sexy songs that had taken the night to even higher heights. Even three days later, she still got goose bumps at the recollection.

She'd hoped to hear from Nathan, but as one night became two, she realized that he wasn't going to contact her. Of course, she had no reason to expect him to reach out. He'd been clear that he wasn't looking for a relationship. The night, as wonderful as it had been, was a one-off. It was the fulfillment of the bargain they'd made at the auction—not the start of a romance. Since she'd only agreed to bid on a bachelor on the condition that it was a onetime thing with no expectation of keeping in touch, she shouldn't feel disappointed.

Though he'd tried to deny it, she knew he had some reservations about her being a single mother. She'd heard the surprise in his voice when she'd mentioned Chloe. Of course, surprise didn't equate to reluctance. She might be reading too much into the tone of his voice.

Not that it mattered. Truth be told, she wasn't in a position to start a relationship. Her little girl needed all of her love and attention. Just caring for Chloe took all of her energy. There was only one of her, and she was pretty tapped out at the moment. And her heart was still too bruised to risk with another man, no matter how good it felt to be around him.

At least that was what she told herself. Now she wondered, if she met the right man, would she be willing to make space for him in her life? Willing to take a chance on loving him. If things had worked out with Owen, she would be in the exact same position—loving her child and loving a man. Of course, in that fantasy world, Owen would have loved his daughter, and her care wouldn't have fallen exclusively on Alexandra.

"And why am I thinking about that now?" Alexandra asked herself.

Chloe splashed the water, getting some of it on Alexandra. Deciding that her daughter had played long enough, Alexandra grabbed soap and a washcloth. Alexandra washed Chloe and then wrapped her squirming child in a towel and carried her into her bedroom and got her dressed for bed. They played until Chloe began to yawn and rub her eyes.

"Story time," Alexandra said, grabbing two books and Chloe's blankie. She sat in the rocker and snuggled her daughter on her lap and began to read. It wasn't long before her Chloe dozed off. Alexandra kissed the top of Chloe's head before she laid her in her crib and tiptoed from the room.

She was trying to figure out which television program to watch when her cell phone rang. Grabbing it, she answered without looking at the display. "Hello."

"Hi. Is this a good time?"

Nathan's deep voice sent shivers down Alexandra's spine. She'd long since given up on hearing from him, so this was a pleasant surprise. Telling herself to be cool, she answered in a voice she hoped didn't betray her excitement. "It's perfect."

"Good. I was just thinking of you and decided to see how you've been doing."

"Funny, I was just thinking about you and how much fun I had Saturday." The honest words popped out of her mouth before she had time to stop them. So much for playing it cool.

"It was a good time. I can't recall the last time I had that much fun."

"Same. You asked how I've been. I've been fine. Things are good at work. Aunt Rose has resumed her life and is as active as ever. Chloe is the sweetest baby in the world. She's even more so now that she is asleep."

Nathan laughed, a rich sound that reverberated through Alexandra. She'd almost forgotten how much she liked his voice and how deeply it affected her.

"So you're enjoying some 'you' time."

"It's like being on vacation." Alexandra laughed.

"I understand that. But you have told me about everyone but you. How are you?"

She blew out a breath. "I'm managing. Getting my feet beneath me."

"Have you decided whether to make the move to Aspen Creek a permanent one?"

"Not yet." She paused. Talking about that wouldn't help her make that decision. She believed the answer would come to her eventually. "How are things on the ranch?"

"Good. I spent most of today working to close a deal in a new market. We've done a lot of preliminary work these past months. Now we're setting a date for an in-person meeting to seal the deal."

"That sounds great. Good luck with that."

"Thanks."

Alexandra tucked her feet beneath her and got comfortable. She and Nathan hadn't known each other very long, but it felt natural to be talking to him at the end of the day.

"You mentioned that you have never been to a ranch."

"Not yet."

"Would you like to visit mine? Seeing it will give you more information about Aspen Creek. You don't want to make a decision without all of the facts."

"I'd love to." Did he think he needed to convince her to visit? She wanted to see the ranch. More than that, she wanted to spend more time with him. No number of reasons why she should keep him at a distance could change that.

"When is a good time for you?"

"I work three twelves—Mondays, Thursdays and Fridays. Any other day works for me."

"How about Saturday afternoon?"

"That's perfect."

"And it goes without saying that your daughter is included in the invitation."

Alexandra's heart warmed at his words. Although she tried to deny it, Owen's rejection of his own child had made her wary of men. A part of her expected each of them to want nothing to do with her daughter, so Nathan's welcoming attitude was a pleasant surprise. Maybe she had read too much into the tone of his voice before.

"Thanks for thinking of her, but Chloe won't be able to attend. One of Aunt Rose's friends is bringing over her granddaughter for a playdate." Alexandra chuckled. "My little girl has quite the social life. Besides, I'm not sure the ranch is the right place for a child."

"You're kidding, right? I grew up on a ranch. It's perfectly safe."

"I suppose. Maybe it's the city girl in me, but I need to check it out first. Just to be on the safe side."

"Since you're a city girl, I'll allow your skepticism."

"Thank you," Alexandra replied, smiling.

"I'll see you then. Good night."

"Good night." Alexandra ended the call and smiled. She was going to see Nathan again.

It was early, so she immediately sent out a group text to her friends.

I just talked to Nathan.—Alexandra

Really?—Kristy

So much for one and done.—Marissa

He must have said something good for you to message us. So spill.—Veronica

He invited me to his ranch.—Alexandra

Wait. I need details. We need to talk.—Kristy

In a minute, they were all on the line, talking over each other.

"One date and he's inviting you to meet the parents? That was fast," Kristy said, laughing. Marissa and Veronica joined in.

"Okay, now you're scaring me," Alexandra said.

"I mentioned wanting to see the ranch. I didn't say a word about meeting his parents."

"We'll stop teasing you. Seriously, that sounds like a good time," Marissa said.

"What are you going to wear?" Kristy, the most fashionable of the friend group, asked.

"Jeans and gym shoes I suppose." She hadn't had much time to think about it.

"Not gym shoes," Veronica said. "Get some cowboy boots."

"And a nice cowboy hat to finish the look," Kristy added. "There's a Western-wear shop in town. They have lots of cute clothes. They have a lot of overpriced touristy stuff in front, but locals get their stuff from the room in the back."

"Get them soon so you can break them in. You don't want to walk around in boots that hurt your feet," Marissa said. "You won't have any fun that way."

"And you won't be nearly as cute either," Kristy added.

"True on both points," Alexandra said. Not that she should be worried about looking cute for Nathan. "How long will it take to break them in?"

"A couple of days should do it," Kristy said.

"I'll go tomorrow."

"What time?" Veronica asked. "I'll take my lunch and we can go together."

"Sounds good. How about noon?"

"Perfect."

"Be sure to send pictures to Marissa and me," Kristy said.

"I will," Alexandra promised.

They said good-night and then ended the call. Alexandra told herself that spending time with Nathan wasn't a big deal.

Her pounding heart let her know she hadn't fooled herself.

Late the next morning, Alexandra got Chloe dressed to go shopping. Despite telling herself not to make a big deal of it, she was excited about the prospect of seeing Nathan again.

Aunt Rose was sitting on the sofa, doing some needlepoint, when Alexandra carried Chloe into the room and put on her jacket. Aunt Rose looked up and smiled. "Where are the two of you going?"

"I'm going to buy some cowboy boots and a cowboy hat."

"What brought this on?"

"Nathan invited me to visit the ranch, and the girls convinced me that I should get boots and a hat."

"That's a good idea. I haven't been to a ranch in ages, but boots are definitely better than regular shoes. After all, you never know what you'll step in."

Alexandra wrinkled her nose. "I hadn't thought of that."

"You aren't going to turn into a wimpy city girl, are you? Surely you're sturdier than that."

Alexandra laughed. "Are you forgetting that I brought two suitcases of designer clothes with me?

Not to mention all the shoes and purses. I am a city girl."

"I haven't forgotten that at all. And since I appreciate good quality clothes, I think that was a good idea. It's easier to take what you want out of your closet than it is to purchase something new in a pinch. But sturdiness has nothing to do with the clothes you wear and everything to do with the kind of person you are inside. You never struck me as the type of woman who would break out in a sweat if she stepped in a little bit of cow poop. Am I wrong?"

"No. I'm a pediatric nurse, remember? I've been thrown up on, bled on, peed on. I don't think there is a bodily fluid that hasn't landed on me at some point."

"Good."

"I'm sure you meant that in a way other than how it sounded."

Aunt Rose laughed. "Don't be so sure. I just might have a mean streak."

Alexandra shook her head. "That's not possible."

Aunt Rose simply smiled mischievously.

After draping Chloe's diaper bag across her shoulder, Alexandra picked up her daughter. "We won't be long."

"You know you can always leave Chloe here with me."

"I know. But I don't want to take advantage. Besides, it's nice outside and she could use a little fresh air."

"You could never take advantage. But I agree about the fresh air. Have a good time."

Alexandra buckled Chloe into her car seat and then headed for downtown Aspen Creek. Aunt Rose's house was in one of the more established residential neighborhoods in town. Each house was large and set on a one-acre lot. Most of Aunt Rose's neighbors were senior citizens, although a couple in their thirties moved in across the street a week ago. The neighbors were friendly and doted on Chloe, but if Alexandra chose to make her move to Aspen Creek permanent, she would have to seriously consider a different area. It would be unfair to raise her daughter in a neighborhood that didn't have kids her age for her to run and play with.

When they reached downtown, Alexandra parked and then got the stroller from the trunk. She strapped Chloe into the stroller and looked up. Veronica was walking down the street.

"Perfect timing," Veronica said as she came to stand beside Alexandra.

"I could have picked you up at the library."

"No need. The library is only two blocks away." Veronica leaned over and tapped Chloe on her nose. "And how is my favorite little baby today?"

Chloe cooed and kicked her legs in response.

"She's having the best day ever," Alexandra answered.

"Does she know how to have any other type?" Veronica asked and then straightened.

"If only you knew," Alexandra joked. Chloe was a good baby, but she still had the occasional bad day.

They reached the Western-wear store and stepped inside. As expected, several tourists were wandering about, trying to find the perfect souvenir. A woman with an elaborately decorated cowboy hat perched on her head was standing in the middle of the room, holding two different fancy boots in her hands, as if trying to decide which pair to buy.

Scooting around the woman, Alexandra and Veronica walked down a narrow hallway to the back of the building. They stepped into a room that was just as well lit as the one in the front. Clearly the owner valued the residents' business as much as he did the vacationers' money. Veronica made a beeline for the earrings on a counter while Alexandra looked at the hats.

A middle-aged salesman approached Alexandra and gave her a friendly smile. "How can I help you?"

"I'm looking for boots and a hat," she replied with a smile of her own.

"Sure. We'll get your feet measured and then you can take a look around. How does that sound?"

"That makes perfect sense to me."

He led her to a row of chairs and then pushed one aside so she could place the stroller beside her.

Alexandra took off her shoes and the salesman quickly measured her feet.

Veronica returned and glanced at the salesman. "Hello, Mr. Carter. How are you doing?"

"I'm just fine, Veronica. How about you?"

"No complaints. This is my friend, Alexandra. She's Rose Kenzie's niece."

"Nice to meet you. And how is Rose doing these days?"

"She's fine. Up to her old tricks."

"Give her my best."

"I will."

Alexandra took Chloe out of the stroller and then headed over to the boots. She looked at a few and then picked up one that she liked.

Veronica picked up a boot and held it up. "What do you think of this one?"

"It's nice." Alexandra held up the boot she held. It was the same style as the one in Veronica's hand. While Veronica had picked up a black boot, Alexandra held a brown one.

"Great minds and all that," Veronica said.

"Clearly."

When Mr. Carter returned, he looked at the boots they held. "I'll be right back with both colors."

Choosing boots proved easier than choosing a hat. There were so many to choose from, each as gorgeous as the next. Although Alexandra didn't expect to wear the boots or hats more than a couple of times, she still wanted to look good. After she'd narrowed it down to two that complemented her face the best, she sought Veronica's opinion.

"The first one," Veronica said.

"Really? I was leaning toward the second."

Veronica took a picture of Alexandra wearing each hat and then texted them to Kristy and Marissa. They immediately texted back. Predictably, the vote was split.

"You could get both," Veronica said.

Alexandra shook her head. "And have two hats that I won't wear more than once? Nope."

"Let Chloe decide. After all, we haven't consulted her."

Veronica was currently holding Chloe, so Alexandra held a hat in each hand and then turned to face her daughter. "Which one do you like best?"

Chloe actually looked at the hats as if she was seriously contemplating the decision. Then she smiled and reached out for the hat in Alexandra's right hand, choosing the hat that Alexandra liked a little bit better.

"That settles it," Veronica said. "Although I still think you'll look great in either one of them."

"The real question is, will Nathan think I look good in it."

"Really? Interesting. Do go on."

Alexandra clapped a hand against her mouth. Had she really just said that? She couldn't believe that she'd actually thought it, much less said it out loud. Nathan's preferences shouldn't be a consideration. "Forget that you heard that."

"You're kidding, right?"

"More like hopeful."

Veronica mimed locking her lips. "Your secret is safe with me."

"Thank you."

Her friend smiled. "I just wonder how long it will be safe with you."

## Chapter Seven

Nathan watched as Alexandra drove through the double gates and onto the paved driveway. She pulled over and stopped to let him get in. He'd offered to drive into Aspen Creek and pick her up, but she'd turned him down, insisting that she could drive herself. He climbed into the passenger seat and fastened his seat belt. The ranch was over fifteen thousand acres, and his house was off the beaten path. It was easier to show her where it was than to give her directions.

"How was your drive?" he asked, taking a moment to look at her. She'd pulled her thick hair into a ponytail at the nape of her neck, giving him a perfect view of her face. Her skin was clear and glowing. Her rich brown eyes were sparkling with excitement. But it was her full lips, parted in a smile, that attracted the majority of his attention. He knew how soft those lips were. How heavenly it was to kiss them, feeling them move beneath his. How sweet she tasted. How easy it would be to be distracted by her presence and do something foolish—like fall for her.

Even knowing the danger she posed to his five-year plan, he hadn't been able to resist calling her. He'd needed to see her again.

"Good. Peaceful," she said.

He forced himself to focus on the conversation, and not the slender legs in tight jeans. "Glad to hear it."

"It really is a straight shot from town. And it's quite scenic. I haven't been out of town since I moved here. I'm beginning to see what I missed."

"We'll make up with some of that today. There are some really scenic spots here. Drive down the driveway until you reach a split in the road, then head to the right."

"Okay."

"My parents' house is straight ahead. I would introduce you to them, but they're spending the day in Denver."

The sound she made was a cross between choking and laughter. He was trying to figure out its meaning, when she spoke. "That sounds like a nice way to spend a Saturday."

"It's nice to see my parents taking it easier now. When my brothers and I were younger, they worked really hard. My brothers and I don't work every day, but back then, my father did. More often than not, my mother was by his side. Dad might not have worked a full day on Sundays, but he still worked a few hours.

When we were older, my brothers and I tried to keep up with him."

He glanced over at her. She was watching the road, but he could tell that she was listening.

"Make a right and then follow the path around the lake," he instructed. The road wasn't paved, but tracks had been worn in the dirt.

"You're right. I never would have found your house."

He nodded.

"What was it like growing up on the ranch?"

He smiled as memories rushed back. "I had a great childhood. My parents never forced us to follow in their footsteps. If one or all of us had chosen other careers, Mom and Dad would have supported us. Despite the fact that my brothers and I have vastly different personalities, we all wanted to be ranchers."

"Does that cause conflict?"

"Occasionally, but not often. Despite our differences, we have a similar outlook on life. And we're close friends. I know Miles and Isaac have my back. And I have theirs."

"Sounds a lot like my family. My brother, sister, and I all look out for each other. Of course we have a tendency to butt into each other's business a little too much."

"As siblings do."

"When we were kids, my brother, Joshua, did all the talking, and my sister, Victoria, and I did all the listening. At some point, she joined him. Now that we're older, it goes in all directions. It's nice to know that they respect my opinion."

She drove around the lake and stopped in front of an impressive house. "Wow."

"You like it?"

"It's breathtaking. And not at all what I was expecting."

"What were you expecting?"

She shrugged. "A log cabin maybe. Or a white clapboard house like in *The Wizard of Oz*. Something more ranch-y. Definitely not something from the pages of *Architectural Digest*."

"A few years back, I built a smaller house. I was gone a lot then, so I let my brother and his ex-wife live there. When I decided to build what I wanted, I decided on this design. I actually like the modern look. Some people might find the glass a bit too much, but I think it fits well with nature. And I get views from every room in the house, which I love."

"I'm not an art critic or architect, but I think it's perfect."

"Wait until you see inside."

Once they were standing beside the car, she leaned against her door and stared at the house with undisguised awe. His parents and brothers had been shocked when he'd shown them the plans for the house. They'd been sure he'd build something more traditional. Something safer. After all, he was by far the most conservative of the brothers. Or, as Isaac liked to say, he was more of a stick-in-the-mud than the others. Nathan didn't deny it. But when it came to his house, he'd wanted something bold. Something that reflected another part of him. The part of him that wanted to step outside the box and be a bit more frivolous. More daring and unpredictable. So he and the architect worked together to design this five-bedroom house of glass, steel, and stone that overlooked the lake.

He led her up the wide stone exterior stairs and through the oversize double glass doors.

"This is something else," she said, as she stood in the two-story foyer, her head back as she looked at the exquisite crystal chandelier. "I don't think I would ever leave for work. It's all so beautiful. I would just stand here and just stare."

"Believe me, I did a lot of that when I first moved in. I couldn't believe that it was my house. Although I was involved in every step of the process, I couldn't imagine how it would feel to stand inside on that first day. Every day I find something new to marvel over."

"I love the finishes you chose. I heard that marble feels cold, but nothing about your house feels cold."

"What would you rather see first, upstairs or the main floor?" Once more he was doing something he never did. He didn't usually invite women to the ranch—they tended to read more into that than he'd intended—and he certainly didn't give them tours of his home. It didn't make sense, yet he couldn't seem to stop himself.

"This is your home, so you should decide what you want to show me and what is off-limits."

"Let's start upstairs." Apparently nothing was off-limits.

He led her up the curved stairway to a wide land-ing. Alexandra looked over the rail, taking in the view from the second floor. "Wow. Again."

Though it shouldn't affect him, her obvious delight with his house stroked his ego. Nathan led her to the far end of the second floor, to his home office. It was quiet and decorated in a minimalist style.

"This is so spartan," Alexandra said.

"I have everything I need. Desk, chair, fridge, and microwave. Get the work done and get out is my motto."

"Does it work?"

"You'd be surprised by how well."

He showed her the four guest suites, each of which had a walk-in closet and a luxurious attached bathroom. The rooms were sunny and spacious with gorgeous views of the ranch from each window.

Alexandra gave him a sweet smile. "Nice. I imagine that you have a hard time getting your guests to leave."

He could have told her that he didn't have guests, so that wouldn't be a problem, but instead he simply nodded. He didn't want to give her the impression that he was cold and unfeeling. Friendless.

Alexandra was stepping into the hallway, so he led her to the last door. His master bedroom. Although she had been nothing but complimentary, Nathan was suddenly worried about what she would think about his bedroom. While he'd paid a designer to decorate the other rooms, he'd done the master bedroom himself. He'd wanted it to be a reflection of himself.

"Is this your sanctuary?" she asked. As usual, Alexandra's eyes sparkled with pleasure, which put him at ease. Not that he should have been uncomfortable in the first place. This was his home after all. He was the only one who had to like it. Even so, he inhaled deeply before swinging open the double doors.

As she had in the other rooms, Alexandra went to the middle of the room and turned in a slow circle, as if trying to absorb the feel of the room into her soul before moving. In the guest rooms, she'd run her hands across the comforters or picked up a random art object to study it. Now she didn't move, letting her eyes do the inspecting. Nathan appreciated that she showed respect for his personal items, but suddenly he didn't want her to keep her distance. He wanted her to feel free to sit on his bed and touch his belongings. Touch him. He wanted her to feel at home.

He shook his head at that thought and tried to push it away. That was going a little too far.

"I like it," she said, pulling his attention back to the here and now.

He blew out a breath, relieved that she had no idea what he'd been thinking. "Thanks."

"I like the colors you chose. They seem to bring in the outside. And of course, the view is outstanding." She crossed to the floor-to-ceiling wall of windows with their view of the lake and the mountains in the distance. "Just waking up to this must put you in the best mood."

"It does." There were nights when he'd lain in his bed and just stared out at the starry sky or across the vast acres of land to the outline of the mountains in the distance. Nothing compared to watching as lightning flashed in the dark sky on stormy nights.

"I'm jealous," she said, a smile belying her words.

"Why?"

"My aunt lives in a great neighborhood, but the views don't compare to this."

"There's no reason to be jealous. Consider this your invitation to visit the ranch anytime you feel like it."

She gave him a look he couldn't interpret and then crossed the room until she was standing near enough for him to touch. His hands ached to reach out and caress the smooth brown skin of her cheek, so he shoved it into his pocket. "You might want to reconsider that statement. For all you know, I might show up one day with my daughter in one arm and my bags in the other. Then where would you be?"

"Good point," he said, but the picture she'd painted held some appeal. Although he was the oldest son, he was the only one without a family of his own. Miles had Jillian, Benji, and Lilliana. They would officially become a family in a week.

Isaac had his sweet baby girl and was engaged to the love of his life. Although he and Savannah hadn't set a date, they were a family in every way that mattered.

Suddenly Nathan felt as if he had fallen behind, which was ridiculous. He was the one who'd set the schedule for his life. He followed his own timeline. He'd created his five-year plan. If he wanted to adjust it, he could at any moment.

That straight in his mind, he showed Alexandra his closet, which was twice the size of the ones in the guest room and then let her explore his bathroom. After she admired the steam shower and soaking tub, they went back down the stairs and returned to the foyer. Once there, he led her through the living room, dining room, den, family room, and finally the kitchen. With each of her exclamations of pleasure, his pride grew.

By the time they stepped onto his back patio, he was nearly bursting. She smiled. "This has to be the best home I've ever been in. And it's not just the architecture, although that is spectacular. I really like how warm and welcoming it feels."

"That's what I was going for. I want it to feel homey."

"You succeeded."

"Now would you like to see the ranch?"

"I would."

He flashed her a grin. "I don't suppose you know how to ride a horse?"

"You are correct. But I'm willing to try if it's necessary."

"Not today. We can make do with a Jeep."

"Okay."

They made small talk as they walked to his garage. Once they were in the Jeep, he drove down the paved road until it ended, turning into gravel and dirt. He slowed so that the uneven road wouldn't jostle her too much.

Alexandra planted a hand on her cowboy hat as

she looked around. Watching her reaction, Nathan realized that he had begun to take the beauty of the ranch for granted. Now he allowed himself to see it anew through her eyes. Without a doubt, the ranch was on the most beautiful land in the country, and he realized just how blessed he'd been to call it home. He could walk for hours, days even, and not leave Montgomery property. He was in the middle of making a deal that would add even more acreage to their ranch.

The Duncan brothers, who owned the adjoining ranch, had finally agreed to sell. It had taken months of extensive, and at times painful, negotiations, but they had finally settled upon terms that made everyone happy. All that was left was to sign the contract.

"Where are your cows?" Alexandra asked.

"Grazing in one of the north pastures. We have to move them often so that they don't overgraze an area. We add supplemental food of course."

"They don't live in barns?"

"Not ordinarily. But we've built breaks to keep them from getting too cold on the range."

"Do you have pigs and chickens? Do you grow corn and beans?"

He shot her a look. "You mean like Old MacDonald?"

She shook her head. Although they were traveling at a slow pace, there was still enough wind to play with her thick, black hair. A few locks blew into her face, and she used her free hand to brush them back behind her ears. "Sort of."

"Yes and no."

"Oh, that's not confusing at all."

He laughed. "Yes, we have chickens. No pigs though. We don't raise them to sell. My mother just likes having fresh eggs. They taste so much better than store-bought. Mom also has a big garden where she grows all kinds of vegetables. Again, for personal consumption. Nothing compares to a salad made with fresh vegetables. We can sneak into her garden and grab enough for a salad for two."

"Oh no. You aren't going to include me in your larceny."

He laughed. "My mother won't mind. She's always giving vegetables to us. She grows more than she and my father could ever eat. And believe me, when it's time to harvest them, she has plenty of eager help."

"Harvest? Just how big is this garden?"

He shrugged. "I don't know. An acre, give or take."

"And she calls it a garden?"

"That's what it is."

"They definitely do some things bigger in ranch country."

"Everything is bigger in ranch country."

She raised an eyebrow, and he realized how suggestive his comment must have sounded. He could have tried to take the words back but didn't. That would only attract more attention to them. Besides, he didn't mind if she thought he was flirting with her. Because he was. "I'll keep that in mind."

"You do that."

He drove over a hill, parked, and they climbed out of the vehicle. The ground was covered in gold wildflowers that whipped in the wind. A stand of tall trees in the middle of the field provided a bit of shade. Birds flew across the sky, chirping and filling the air with their songs. Squirrels and rabbits darted across the grass, as if disturbed by Nathan's and Alexandra's presence. In the distance a few deer drank from a babbling brook.

"I love it here. It looks like something out of a fairy tale," Alexandra whispered, as if speaking too loudly would ruin the enchantment.

"It's one of my favorite places on the ranch. I thought about building my house here, but somehow it seemed wrong. Intrusive. As if I would be defiling something beautiful. I like to come here and soak up the atmosphere. Then I leave it, as perfect as I found it."

"You generally don't drive here, do you?"

He shook his head. "No. I usually come here on horseback. But I made an exception because I wanted to show it to you." He didn't want to give too much thought to why it had been so important to share this place with her. The answer might not align with his five-year plan.

And he wasn't ready to adjust that just yet.

Alexandra tried to keep her delight at his words under control. After all, she wasn't looking for a relationship. Neither was he. So why was she having such difficulty remembering that? And why was it so easy to imagine herself—and Chloe—spending more time here with Nathan? Whatever the reason, it ended now. She wasn't going to let her feelings lead her into possible heartbreak. She was going to stick to more general topics.

"I had a few preconceived notions about the ranch. None of them have proven to be accurate."

"Like what?"

He sounded genuinely interested so she answered honestly. "Well, for one, I thought that animals would be a lot closer to your house. Like I would walk out the back door and encounter bulls and cows."

"That could be true on some ranches. Especially smaller ones. Well, maybe not that close, but certainly closer than here. And given the time of year, our cattle might actually be grazing closer to the houses."

"And I thought that it would…smell. You know, like the zoo, only a million times worse."

He threw back his head and laughed. She liked the sound it made as it echoed across the vast acres. It was bold and robust, as confident as the man she was coming to know. "You know, there is a certain smell to nature that you get used to over time. If you would like a more up close and personal view of the ranch more in line with what you pictured, including the smells, we can do that."

"Would you think that I was weird if I said yes?"

"No. I want today to be everything you imagined it would be."

They traipsed back down the hill and climbed back into the Jeep. This was such a new experience for her and she was enjoying it more than she'd expected. She'd seen some of the most famous tourist attractions in the world and amazingly the ranch ranked up there with them. Perhaps it was the handsome tour guide showing her around that made the day so special.

He certainly was holding her attention. He'd looked incredibly dapper in his suit the night of the auction but dressed in jeans that fit his muscular thighs perfectly, and a plaid shirt that hugged his sculpted torso, he looked even more appealing. Just looking at him made her mouth water and stirred up longings she didn't want to feel. She used to believe that it was okay to look as long as she didn't touch. That didn't apply in Nathan's case. Looking at him was dangerous. Especially when she wasn't sure she could stop at just looking. Nor was she certain that she wanted to.

As they rode across the grassy hills and valleys, Nathan entertained her with amusing stories about growing up on a cattle ranch. He and his brothers had learned early on that the cattle weren't pets, nor was it safe for them to forget that the huge animals could crush and kill them in mere minutes.

"Did you ever ignore the rules and do something dangerous?"

"Like what?"

"I don't know…walk along the fence rail where the cattle were?"

He shook his head and gave her a quick look. They were driving across the grass and there was no danger of them running into another vehicle. "No. You forget, I'm the oldest brother. When my parents weren't around, I was responsible for keeping Miles and Isaac safe. I couldn't very well do something dangerous when I knew that one or both of them would mimic my behavior at a later date."

"Did you ever want to do something crazy or risky?"

"No. Maybe it's a result of being the oldest, but I never could forget that I had to be a role model." One side of his lips lifted in a quirk and her stomach gave a silly little lurch in response. Nathan was objectively handsome, so naturally she would enjoy looking at his gorgeous face and muscular body. There was nothing worrisome about that. But when her body started to react like a schoolgirl with a crush? Then it was time to dial it back. Fast.

She'd already made one mistake with Owen. True, she'd been more than physically attracted to him. They'd spent a lot of time together and she'd liked the person that he'd appeared to be. He had talked for hours about helping the less fortunate in their communities as well as around the world. All appearances indicated that he'd been sincere. He donated to worthy causes and even helped establish a nonprofit to help homeless youth find homes, get GEDs and jobs.

But that generous spirit had only been a facade. A way of sanitizing his otherwise dirty interior. He hadn't really cared about people. Not really. He'd only been concerned as long as he was able to keep them at a distance. Or in a situation where he could maintain an air of superiority. His heart hadn't extended to love for his own child.

And why was she thinking about Owen now when she was in the company of this charming man? Oh yeah, *because* he was charming. She needed to remind herself not to make the same mistake with Nathan. She couldn't allow herself to get swept away by his charm and good looks. Even if he was truly as wonderful as he appeared, a relationship was the last thing she needed right now. Not that Nathan had given any indication that he was looking to start a romance with her. He hadn't once hinted about today being anything more than it was—an opportunity for her to see his ranch up close.

True, he'd flirted with her earlier, but it had seemed spontaneous, not something that was part of a playbook. And that made him even more appealing to her. But she needed to slow down. In fact, she needed to *stop*. She wasn't looking for a relationship. That was one of the reasons she'd been eager to move to this small town. To her way of thinking, the odds that she would meet someone she found attractive had been a million to one. Now it looked like her math had been off a bit.

Alexandra heard the sound of the lowing before she saw the cattle. She inhaled, and her nostrils were filled with their odor. She coughed. With each passing second, the odor and the noise grew even stronger.

Nathan stopped the Jeep and turned to her. "We can get out here and walk the rest of the way if you want."

She felt a bit of trepidation. "They aren't going to charge us, are they?"

"What? Not up for that kind of adventure?"

"No. I'm wearing boots, not gym shoes. I'm sure

they'll slow me down." She held up her leg so he could see her boots.

"Those are nice. They look new."

"They are. I got them especially for this visit."

"Did you now?"

"Yes. I'm hoping that I can get more use out of them. I won't be able to wear them at work, and to be honest, I haven't been to many places where women were wearing boots."

"Where have you been?" he asked as they walked toward the cattle.

"Not too many places. You already know about my dinner at Bliss on Your Lips. My friends and I have treated ourselves to dinner at a few other fancy restaurants. That's it."

"I see. Well, you're getting some use out of them now. I don't know a lot about women's fashion, but I imagine you can wear them to the grocery store. Or running errands."

"I suppose."

They'd reached the fences surrounding the cattle. The cows were eating the grass and milling around. There was lots of room for the animals to move which she was pleased to see. Although she didn't consider herself to be an animal activist, she did care about the living conditions of the animals that would become the food she ate. She wanted them to have a good quality of life. Apparently Nathan and his family felt the same way.

Nathan held out his hand and she took it as if it was the most natural thing in the world to do. They swung their hands as they approached the cattle. He stopped at a safe distance and then they just watched for a while without talking. It was nice. This was different from the way she'd spent most of her Saturday afternoons when she'd lived in Chicago. It was even different from the way she'd been spending her free time since she moved to Aspen Creek.

And she enjoyed it. The weather was warm and the sky was clear. There was something soothing about standing quietly and watching the cows.

She wondered how Chloe would react to seeing the animals. Would she delight in listening to them moo? A part of her wondered if she should have taken Nathan up on his invitation to include her in the day. But that might prove risky. She didn't want Chloe to get attached to someone who wasn't going to be a permanent part of their lives. Since neither she nor Nathan was looking for a relationship, things between them were temporary. It would be best for her to keep Nathan at a distance until she had a better handle on things. He hadn't even met Chloe yet. Perhaps that was for the best.

After she'd had her fill of looking at the cattle—and being downwind of them—she suggested that they stroll around for a bit. It was all so scenic and so peaceful. So isolated. It was as if they were the only two people in the world.

That thought stopped her in her tracks. She'd learned the hard way that fantasy and reality rarely intersected. *Once upon a time* was not the way relationships began in real life. Now that she was a mother, she needed to keep both of her feet firmly on the ground. She couldn't set her child up for the heartbreak of disappointment.

"I suppose I need to get going," Alexandra said after a while. The day had been wonderful, but she didn't want to overstay her welcome. Besides, Chloe was at home. She needed to spend some time with her.

Nathan looked surprised and for a long moment he didn't speak. A part of her wanted him to protest, to insist that she stay longer, but the rational part of her hoped he wouldn't. She didn't know if she was strong enough to resist his appeal for much longer. She needed to create some distance from him so she could remind herself why she didn't want a man in her life right now.

"Okay. Let's get you back to your car."

"I had the best time. Thank you so much for inviting me."

"You're more than welcome."

They got back into the Jeep and drove over the field. Nathan took a different way back to his house, showcasing even more beautiful spots. She saw a few men in the distance, but other than waving, Nathan paid no attention to them. The drive went quickly, and Alexandra was actually sad when his house came into view. He parked and then they turned and faced each other.

She sighed. "I suppose I need to get out of your Jeep."

"We both do. I left my motorcycle at the front gate, so I'll ride back with you."

"You have a motorcycle?"

He nodded. "Surprised?"

"Totally." She grinned at him. "You're more fun than you let on."

He winked. "Let's keep that between the two of us. I have a reputation as a stick-in-the-mud to uphold."

Alexandra burst out laughing. "Your secret is safe with me."

They got out of the Jeep and into her car to ride back to the front gate. When they arrived, he didn't get out of the car. Instead, he looked at her as if debating with himself. Since she had internal battles quite often, she waited patiently until he appeared to reach a decision.

"My brother is getting married next week."

That was not at all what she was expecting him to say. She nodded. "I remember. You told me. That's a good thing. Right?"

"Yes. I'm happy for them. It's just my mother. She's caught up in the whole romance thing. It's only my two brothers and me. Now my mother has wedding fever. She thinks we all need to settle down. Miles is getting married. Isaac is engaged. And then there's me."

"Don't tell me she's matchmaking."

He gave her a look that spoke volumes.

"Yikes."

"That about sums it up. She's on a mission. Before she was too busy helping Miles with Benji and worrying about Isaac's revolving door of women, to do more than throw a random woman in my direction. But that's all changed. I'm the sole focus of her attention. I'm afraid to answer my door for fear that she'll be standing there with a single woman by her side."

"Now you're exaggerating."

"Maybe a little. But she's on a mission. Last Sunday, she asked about our date."

"How did she know we went out?"

"My mother knows everything. I made the mistake of telling her how good a time we had. I could see the wheels turning in her head. She was just thrilled at the idea of adding another daughter-in-law to the family. When I told her nothing was going to happen between us, she wasn't happy. Especially when I told her that it was mutual. The next thing I knew, she was mentioning some friend's daughter. I tell you, she's not going to rest until she has me in a relationship."

"So what are you going to do?"

"The only thing I can do." He paused. "I'm running away from home."

Laughter burst out of Alexandra's lips. "You are hilarious."

"Desperate is more like it. You would be too if you knew my mother."

"I would help you if I could. I suppose I could write her a letter and ask her to give you a reprieve."

"I wish that would work. No, the only thing that will get her off my case is if she sees me with a woman." He paused, and now she could hear the wheels in *his* head turning. He spoke slowly. "Are you busy next Saturday?"

"No." The word sounded normal, not betraying the caution she felt. "Why?"

"Do you want to go to my brother's wedding with

me? I need someone to keep my mother off my back for a few hours."

She laughed. "That's some kind of invitation. No wonder your mother is worried about you ever having a girlfriend."

He gave her a sheepish grin. "I guess that didn't come across as smooth."

"Not even slightly."

"Well, let me see if I can do it better the second time." He cleared his throat and then spoke in a sexy voice that a radio DJ would envy. "Alexandra. If you are free this Saturday, I would be honored if you accompanied me to my brother's wedding."

Despite knowing that he was only putting on, the timbre of his voice set butterflies free in her stomach. She wouldn't stand a chance if he ever decided to woo her for real. She couldn't let him have all the fun, so she injected her voice with a double dose of sex appeal. "Nathan. I would love to be your date for your brother's wedding. What time should I expect you?"

There was a brief pause before he responded. "The ceremony starts at two. I'll pick you up at noon if that works for you."

"That's fine. I'm looking forward to meeting your family." She realized how that came out and hastened to clarify her statement. "In a general way. Not that I'm hoping to become a part of it."

"I didn't think you did."

"I love weddings," she added, just to be on the safe side.

"That's good." He inhaled and then blew the breath

out slowly. His Adam's apple bobbed up and down twice. "But more than being my date. I need you to pretend to be my girlfriend."

"Oh." She was too shocked to cover the wariness in her voice. "What would that involve?"

He shrugged one of his massive shoulders and looked slightly embarrassed. "I guess just act like you like me."

That wouldn't be hard because she did like him. Perhaps too much. But since neither of them were looking for romance, this could work to her advantage too. She might not want a boyfriend, but she wasn't opposed to having a male friend to spend time with occasionally. Having a make-believe boyfriend might be fun.

It had been a long time since she'd had fun. Aunt Rose was right. She needed more in her life than work and Chloe. Alexandra couldn't suppress a grin. She loved a good caper. "I can hardly wait."

## Chapter Eight

Alexandra checked her appearance in the mirror before going downstairs to wait for Nathan. This was the first wedding she'd attended in a long time. Although her relationship with Owen had ended disastrously, and she was not interested in trying again, she loved weddings and all the trappings. She liked seeing the bridesmaids' dresses and their bouquets. She was always excited to see the bride's wedding dress. Her heart always beat a little faster as she listened to the emotionally spoken wedding vows. There was something so hopeful about witnessing a happy couple promise to love each other forever. If only she didn't know what could go wrong if they didn't keep those promises.

But what she was really looking forward to was seeing Nathan again. No matter how hard she tried to convince herself that this was subterfuge and not a real date, her heart still sped up with the realization that she was going to be spending the next few hours with him.

That feeling was in direct opposition to her plan to avoid romantic entanglements at all costs. But there was something about Nathan that made sticking to her plan next to impossible. Lucky for her, he had no problem sticking to his five-year plan. He was so determined not to be roped into a relationship that he was willing to bring a pretend date to his brother's wedding.

No, that wasn't accurate. She wasn't his pretend date. She was his real date—just not his real girlfriend. His plus one for the reception. She wouldn't lie—especially not to his mother—but if her presence gave people the impression that Alexandra and Nathan were a couple, well she couldn't be responsible for that. She was helping Nathan out of a tight spot. Helping him convince his mom that he didn't need a matchmaker after all.

She just needed to make sure that *she* didn't start to believe there was something romantic between them.

She turned from side to side, then made a minor adjustment to the bottom of her pomegranate-red dress. It was fitted from shoulders to just above her hips, hugging her breasts and waist before flaring out over her knees. It was perfect for an afternoon wedding and reception.

Alexandra had taken extra time with her hair and makeup, and she looked good, if she did say so herself. She went downstairs, where Chloe was on all fours and Crystal was chasing her around the room.

"I'm going to catch you," Crystal said, making Chloe laugh.

Aunt Rose was sitting on the sofa. She smiled and shook her head.

Crystal looked up when Alexandra entered the room. "Wow. You look really pretty."

"Thank you." Alexandra smiled then scooped up Chloe, planting a big kiss on her cheek.

"I bet all of the men will want to dance with you," Crystal continued.

"I don't know about that."

"My dad might. He's going to the wedding. He doesn't have a date, so if he asks you to dance, you should say yes."

Alexandra wondered if Crystal's dad had any idea how much matchmaking Crystal did on his behalf. "I most certainly will. Don't forget, I have Chloe's food and bottles all set up."

"You told me already. And I know when to give her a snack and which ones she likes best."

Alexandra smiled. "You really are a great baby-sitter."

Crystal beamed. "Thank you."

Chloe pushed against Alexandra's chest, straining to get down so she could resume her game of chase. Sighing, Alexandra set her on the floor and then watched as Chloe began crawling around the room while Crystal followed behind her. The doorbell rang and Alexandra hurried to open it. Nathan was standing there, dressed in a black tuxedo, and her heart stuttered. She couldn't tear her eyes away.

"Whoa. You are absolutely gorgeous," Nathan said. His eyes swept over her body, male appreciation in his eyes. Although he hadn't touched her, his gaze had been so hot and intense that her body began to burn.

She told herself that he was just playing a part—after all, she was his pretend girlfriend—but her heart and brain didn't seem to be communicating. Her foolish heart wished he'd been sincere.

"Thank you. And might I add that you look pretty dapper yourself?"

Before she could stop herself, she reached out and straightened his bow tie. When she realized just how intimate that act was, she pulled her hands away and folded them in front of her. There was no reason to pretend when their intended audience wasn't around to see.

He struck a pose, something completely out of character, and winked. "I'm one of the groomsmen, so I had to wear this tux. But we need to get to the resort now."

"Okay."

Chloe crawled over and grabbed a fistful of the cuff of Nathan's pants. Immediately Alexandra leaned over and picked her up. "Sorry about that."

"Don't be." Nathan gave Chloe a long look. He appeared slightly stunned and his voice sounded different. Strained. "This must be your little girl."

"Yes. This is Chloe."

Nathan grinned. "She's a little cutie."

Chloe reached a hand to Nathan, and Alexandra took a step back before her daughter could touch him. "Her hands are a bit grubby. The last thing I want is for her to mess up your tux."

Crystal came over and took Chloe into her arms.

"Thank you. I'll see you later." Alexandra grabbed her wrap and purse from the bench in the hallway and then waved to Aunt Rose and Crystal, blew a kiss to Chloe, and she and Nathan left. She didn't know what to make of Nathan's reaction to Chloe. He had said all of the right things, but something had been off. But then, no doubt he had a lot on his mind with the wedding and was a bit stressed. And first meetings were always a bit strained, so she decided not to make too much of it.

When they were inside his sedan, she turned to him. "Which resort are we going to?"

"I forgot, you're still getting to know Aspen Creek. Jillian—the bride's—family owns one of the most successful resorts in Colorado. They host weddings throughout the year. Miles and Jillian's wedding will be there, of course."

"That sounds wonderful. I imagine it will be quite beautiful."

"As are all the weddings held there. Of course, I know they pulled out all the stops for this one."

"Forget being a rancher, you should have been a tour guide. What else can you tell me about Aspen Creek?"

Nate laughed. "What do you want to know?"

"Anything. Everything. You grew up here, right?"

"Technically, yes, although I really grew up on the ranch. The town is a lot different than it was back then. It wasn't the tourist destination that it is now. The locals all knew about the skiing and outdoor activities, but it was a much smaller place in those days. Very tight-knit. Even those of us who grew up on ranches felt like we belonged."

"That sounds nice."

"It was. Even though the town has grown over the years, it still feels the same. I'm not sure how it happened, but about ten years ago, Aspen Creek went from being Colorado's best-kept secret to an overnight vacation destination of the rich and famous. Now tourists from all over the world vacation here. Aspen Creek is home to many former winter Olympians. They teach skiing, skating, and other things."

"Really? Maybe I'll take a lesson. It would be nice to learn something from the best. What lessons have you taken?"

He shrugged. "Over the years? Skiing. Ice-skating. Snowboarding. Everything they offer."

"Nice. What did you and your friends do for fun?"

"When you live on a ranch, there is a lot of horseback riding. We also skied, went ice-skating, and snowmobiling in the winter. In the summer we met up at the local swimming hole. Or fished and hiked. Everything you can think of, we did."

"You actually had a swimming hole?"

"Yeah."

"Why? I mean, I saw your swimming pool. Didn't your parents have one?"

"Yes. But there was something special about the swimming hole. Maybe the absence of parents was the draw. All of our friends would meet there. We'd hang out for hours. On cool evenings we'd build a bonfire, play music, and dance. Or sit around and talk. Now that I'm older I appreciate having a heated pool in my backyard."

"You can definitely get more use out of it."

"You would think. But I put in so many hours at work that I don't get to swim as much as I used to. I do spend a lot of time in the hot tub though." He glanced at her. "Feel free to come over and use it at any time."

"That's pretty far to go just to sit in your hot tub."

"You'd also get to enjoy the pleasure of my company."

"There is that. But I work full-time. I have a little girl and I need to spend time with her."

"I have nothing against kids. You are more than welcome to bring her with you."

"Really?" Alexandra's heart warmed at Nathan's words. He'd said something similar before, but she'd tried to convince herself that he was being polite. Maybe he hadn't been. Still, she had her reservations about letting Chloe spend a lot of time with Nathan. This charade wasn't going to last forever. Eventually Nathan's mother would cease her matchmaking and he wouldn't need her around. Alexandra would understand his absence, but Chloe wouldn't. Even so, his attitude was a wonderful surprise. Owen hadn't been interested in Chloe, so Alexandra hadn't expected Nathan to be interested either. "Of course, she probably wouldn't want to spend time in the hot tub."

"No. I suppose not. But my invitation to bring her to the ranch still stands."

"I'll keep that in mind."

They arrived at the resort a few minutes later. Nathan parked, then helped Alexandra from the car. Alexandra took one look around and gasped. The view was absolutely breathtaking. She'd never seen anything as scenic. The mountains soared over the resort, appearing to reach the clear blue sky. The trees surrounding the enormous stone building were filled with twinkling white lights. Large urns filled with roses were spaced along the winding path and up the stairs leading to the wide double doors. It was quite romantic, and she couldn't wait to see how the interior had been decorated. No doubt, it was even more romantic.

"Where is the wedding going to be held?"

"In the rooftop chapel. Miles and Jillian had wanted a small, intimate ceremony. Then the parents—or rather the mothers—got involved, and the guest list grew. Now there will be close to a hundred people attending."

Alexandra laughed. "That could still be considered intimate, since it's a wedding."

"That's what the mothers keep saying."

"I hope your brother and his fiancée are okay with the way things ended up. This is their day after all."

"Miles couldn't care less what they do. He's said on more than one occasion that all he wants is to be married to Jillian. Whatever makes her happy makes him happy. And Jillian is no shrinking violet. She'd speak up if she didn't like something. At the end of the day, this will be her dream wedding."

They reached the chapel, and a tuxedoed usher handed them a folded program before they stepped inside. Alexandra looked around and smiled. It was even more beautiful than she'd expected. Every surface was covered with vases filled with pink and white roses. There had to be thousands of them, filling the air with wonderful perfume. Gleaming crystal chandeliers hung from the high ceiling. Rows of chairs covered with white linen and pink bows were divided by a wide aisle. Vases of flowers lined the aisle. An enormous rose-covered arch stood at the front of the room. Alexandra couldn't hold back her sigh. The entire room was a vision.

But as gorgeous as the chapel was, it was the view from behind the floral arch that took her breath away. The floor-to-ceiling windows provided an unobstructed view of the snowcapped mountains. This was the perfect backdrop for a wedding.

"Are you taking notes for your own wedding?" Nathan joked.

Alexandra shook her head, ensuring that the ludicrous notion couldn't take root. "No. Marriage isn't in my plan. You know that. But I'm not above admiring perfection when I see it."

Nathan glanced around. "It is rather nice."

"*Nice* doesn't come close to describing this room."

He shrugged. "What can I say? I'm not the romantic in the family. Remember, I'm the one who's all business all the time."

Alexandra smiled. He might want other people to believe that—he might even believe it himself—but she thought he was selling himself short. There was more to Nathan than business. He was kind and generous. Funny and playful. Thoughtful and considerate. Nathan possessed so many admirable traits that she couldn't begin to name them all. "I'll keep that in mind."

"Do you want to find a seat or would you rather hang out in the lobby? I need to meet up with Miles and the other groomsmen. I hope that's okay with you."

"It's fine. I'll just hang out in the lobby for a bit. I'll go inside a little closer to the start of the ceremony."

Nathan stared at her for a moment, his dark gaze unreadable. A spark of something she couldn't name arced between them and her knees weakened. Then he shook his head, gave her shoulder a gentle squeeze, and left. Alexandra stared at his retreating back, not breathing until he'd disappeared around a corner.

After a while, wedding guests began to arrive, so Alexandra went inside and found a seat near the center of the room.

Minutes later, a middle-aged couple approached Alexandra and the woman spoke. "Would you mind if we joined you?"

"That would be wonderful." Alexandra stood aside so the couple could enter.

"Are you saving a seat for anyone?"

"No. Feel free to sit next to me."

"Thank you." They sat down and then pulled out their phones. The woman stood up and took a few pictures of the chapel. When she was satisfied that she had a shot of everything, she put her phone back into her purse and then turned to Alexandra. "We're Richard and Jerilyn Brown. We know the bride and the groom. Their mothers are two of my dearest friends. I can't tell you how happy we are to see Miles and Jillian get married. Aren't we, Richard?"

Richard had been sneaking looks at what appeared to be some sporting event on his phone, but he managed a nod. "Yes, we are."

Jerilyn rolled her eyes. Clearly she wasn't fooled for a moment. Then she looked at Alexandra, an expectant expression on her face. Not sure what she was supposed to say, Alexandra smiled. Jerilyn sighed. "How do you know the bride and groom?"

"I don't really. I moved to Aspen Creek several months ago. But I know Nathan, the groom's brother. He invited me as his date."

"Really? How long have you and Nathan been dating?"

Alexandra was glad that she and Nathan had anticipated this line of questioning and had prepared an answer. Even so, she was still caught a bit off guard. She hadn't expected to be confronted by the first wedding guest she encountered. Alexandra decided to use this conversation as a trial run. It was a good opportunity to fill in any gaps in the cover story.

Alexandra turned in her seat to better face Jerilyn.

She noted that while Richard was still looking at his phone, he was also listening to the conversation. Apparently gossiping was a gender-neutral sport. "Nathan and I haven't been dating long at all. We met at the Bachelor Auction. I actually won a date with him."

"Don't tell me that he decided to use this as the date." Jerilyn shook her head in disgust and then harrumphed. "That man had better get his head out of the ranch business. Now, his brother, Isaac, has always been a favorite with the ladies. He has enough charm for two people. Nathan could learn a thing or two from him."

"I don't know about Isaac or his charm. But this isn't our date," Alexandra said, quick to correct the older woman and defend Nathan's honor. "Nathan took me to dinner at Bliss On Your Lips and then to Grady's for music and dancing."

"Really." Jerilyn smiled, clearly impressed. Alexandra didn't know why it was important to her that the other woman have a good opinion of Nathan, but it mattered. Jerilyn's friendly smile turned sly. "You must be pretty special for him to take you to such an expensive restaurant on a first date. That's certainly not his style."

"Perhaps Nathan was just waiting for the right woman to come along," Richard chimed in. He patted his wife's hand. "Like I did."

Jerilyn's light brown cheeks pinkened, and she giggled like a schoolgirl. "Oh you."

Richard kissed her cheek and then turned his attention back to his phone.

Alexandra smiled, grateful that Richard had interrupted the conversation. She knew that the other woman meant no harm, and Nathan probably wouldn't care a whit about the other woman's opinion of him. But *she* cared. She decided to change the subject. "How long have you been married?"

"Thirty-two years."

"That's nice." It always filled Alexandra's heart with joy to see happily married couples. Especially ones that had stood the test of time. They worked to balance the disappointment she felt whenever she thought of her failed relationship. Knowing that love could actually last a lifetime tempered the pain she'd experienced.

"Does attending this wedding give you ideas about your future with Nathan?"

Where did that come from? Apparently she hadn't changed the subject as completely as she'd hoped. "It's kind of early for that kind of decision. After all, Nathan and I are still getting to know each other."

"It doesn't always take a long time to know when you've found the right one. It didn't take me long to know that Richard was the one for me. I took one look at him across the diner and that was all it took. I was a goner. I knew I would love him forever. Of course, it took him a bit longer."

"Really? How much longer?" Alexandra loved a good how-I-met-my-spouse story and could listen to them for hours. Especially if it took the heat off her and Nathan.

"Two hours."

"Oh, you have to tell me everything."

Jerilyn looked at her watch and then back at Alexandra. "We have a few minutes before the ceremony is scheduled to start, so why not? I was at the diner with two of my friends. It was the summer before my senior year of college. He had graduated from college the year before and had moved to Aspen Creek to manage his uncle's music venue.

"The instant that I saw him, I was intrigued. Neither of my friends knew who he was, so I decided to find out. I walked up to the bar, where he was studying the dessert menu and told him that the chocolate brownie with whipped cream was my favorite. He nodded but didn't say anything. When my food came, I returned to my table and my friends. I was a bit disappointed that he hadn't asked for my number."

"I bet."

"My friends and I were just finishing our dinners when the waiter brought over three desserts. Chocolate brownies with whipped cream. He said it was courtesy of my friend at the bar. I looked up, but he was gone. The waiter slipped me a note from Richard. I still have that letter to this day. It read: *Thank you for the dessert recommendation. If you don't have a boyfriend and would like to get to know me, please call.* He'd written his telephone number. I called him as soon as I got home."

Alexandra sighed. "Wow. That is so perfect."

"It really was. I practically swallowed my brownie

whole. Then I raced home and called him. We got married three months later."

"That's a beautiful story." One Alexandra couldn't relate to. Although she and Owen had seemed to hit it off right away, it hadn't lasted. How wonderful must it feel to have a relationship last for years. To survive the ups and downs that life threw at you. How sweet it must feel to recognize the person meant for you on sight.

Could love at first sight be real? Alexandra hadn't given it much thought, but she supposed that it could exist in one form or another. She might be a romantic at heart, but she was also a realist. Maybe even a bit of a skeptic when it came to things like that. Even so, she wondered if there was a man she could fall in love with. If not at first sight, maybe after a few sightings.

*How about Nathan?*

That thought came from out of nowhere, startling her. Before she could try it on for size, the pianist began playing, indicating the start of the ceremony. While Alexandra and Jerilyn had been speaking, more guests had begun to arrive and talk quietly. Now a hush came over the room.

Alexandra turned to face the front just as the robed minister and the groom, who looked quite handsome in his tuxedo, stepped into the room and stood before the floral arch. Alexandra's attention was then drawn to Nathan, who was standing beside his brother. Although Miles was the groom, it was Nathan who attracted and held her attention.

She'd seen him in the tuxedo earlier, but that hadn't

made her immune to the impact his appearance had on her. The jacket was tailored to fit his broad shoulders and then tapered to his trim waist. The pants fit his muscular thighs before coming to rest on his shiny black dress shoes. His posture was erect, befitting a man of his presence. It was impossible to tear her eyes away.

There was no sense denying the obvious. Alexandra stared down at her clasped hands. Then she looked up at Nathan, who turned at that moment to glance at her. Their eyes met and held. He smiled and her heart skipped a beat. Incredibly, the other people in the room seemed to disappear and the music faded to nothingness. It was as if Alexandra and Nathan were the only two people in the world.

That feeling shook her to her core and her palms began to sweat. There was no way she was going to start fantasizing about Nathan. Especially after he'd been perfectly clear that there was no romance in their future. He was focused on accomplishing his five-year plan for the ranch. She was fine with that. Especially since she wasn't the least bit interested in giving her heart to anyone.

The romantic atmosphere must be getting to her and playing havoc with her emotions. Weddings, with their love songs and floral arrangements, were romantic by design. Love was being celebrated, so naturally her thoughts would travel down that path. Once she was in her normal environment, the foolish thoughts would vanish into thin air.

She felt a poke in the side and turned to see Jerilyn

smiling at her. "You can fool some of the people in here, but you can't fool me. I can see what's going on between you and Nathan. You can't keep your eyes off each other."

Alexandra's mouth fell open as she tried to think of a suitable response. Nothing came to mind. Perhaps she not only fooled Jerilyn into thinking she and Nathan were dating. She had fooled herself.

"Don't worry. Your secret is safe with me." Jerilyn smiled and then winked. "For now."

The procession began and Alexandra turned her attention to the middle aisle. As she watched the wedding party enter, she tried to get a grip on her suddenly turbulent emotions. She couldn't fall for Nathan. That was a heartbreak waiting to happen.

She smiled as the flower girl and ring bearer walked down the aisle. The little girl looked positively angelic in her frilly dress and the little boy looked charming in his tuxedo.

When the wedding march played, Alexandra joined the others and stood as she watched the bride enter on her father's arm. Even from a distance, Alexandra could feel the happiness radiating from the other woman. Jillian's smile was luminous, and there was a look of unmistakable joy on her face. Alexandra had never seen a more beautiful bride.

Despite warning herself of the dangers of getting swept up in the moment, the entire ceremony was just too beautiful and emotional for her to remain a dispassionate observer. Alexandra's heart overflowed as the bride and groom recited the vows they had written themselves. When Miles and Jillian jumped over the broom and then kissed, Alexandra rose to her feet, applauding with the rest of the guests. Overcome by emotion, she felt her eyes fill with tears, but swiped them away before they could stain her cheeks.

As the bridal party recessed down the aisle, Alexandra tried not to stare at Nathan, but she couldn't pull her gaze away. He still had the proud and happy expression on his face he'd worn as he'd watched his brother get married. He was obviously close to his family. Their relationship reminded her of the one she shared with her siblings.

"That was truly beautiful," Jerilyn said, stirring Alexandra from her musings.

"It truly was," Alexandra agreed easily. "They are so obviously in love. It's so easy to picture them living happily-ever-after."

"Yes. But they took the long and winding road to get here."

"What do you mean?" The bridal party had returned and were now standing at the front of the room. The ushers were at the back of the room, directing the guests row by row to go to greet the couple. The usher had not reached them, so Jerilyn and Alexandra had time to talk.

"Jillian and Miles dated for years. Everyone expected them to get married right out of college. But they didn't. At least not to each other." She waved her hand as if the detail was too insignificant to be of any concern.

Alexandra nodded, indicating that she was following the story.

"Well, neither Miles's nor Jillian's marriages lasted. But—did you notice the ring bearer and the flower girl?"

"Yes. They are so adorable."

"Aren't they? Well, Benji is Miles's son, and Lilliana is Jillian's daughter. So when they got back together, they got a little something extra. Now they're one happy family."

"That's so romantic," Alexandra said honestly. And it gave her hope. Not that she was carrying a torch for Owen. She wouldn't take him back even if he came with a lifetime supply of chocolate. But it was nice to see that people who belonged together eventually ended up together. It was nice to see that there was a way back and that one mistake—even one as big as marrying the wrong person—hadn't been able to stop true love.

The usher came up and directed them to join the line greeting the happy couple. When Alexandra reached the bridal party, she smiled and said hello. Nathan smiled when he reached him and brushed her hand gently. The slight touch was enough to send shivers dancing down her spine. This wedding was definitely playing havoc with her emotions. It was a good thing that she and Nathan had been clear about their intentions. They were only pretending to date in order to keep his mother off his case.

For the first time, she admitted that she could very

easily fall in love with him. The thought was shocking, and she felt her knees weaken.

She somehow managed to get hold of herself enough to murmur "congratulations" to the bride and groom before returning to her seat. After the receiving line ended, Nathan joined Alexandra. She smiled up at him, trying to slow her rapidly beating heart.

"The bridal party took a lot of pictures yesterday and some before the ceremony, but the photographer still wants to take more before we move on to the reception. Do you mind waiting?"

"Not at all. I'll just sit here."

"Thanks." He flashed her a grin before returning to stand before the arch. The two photographers took numerous pictures of the wedding party before dismissing all but the bride and groom.

Nathan approached her once again, a smile on his face. As he drew nearer, Alexandra couldn't help but admire his handsome face and muscular body. It was indisputable that he was one of the most attractive men she had ever known. There was something about his aura that wouldn't allow her to resist him for any length of time.

When he was standing beside her, he reached out a hand. She took it and rose. His fingers were warm and strong as they wrapped around hers. There was unmistakable power in his grip.

"Where is the reception going to be held?"

"The resort has a beautiful ballroom."

"It can't possibly be more beautiful than this."

"Maybe. Maybe not. I'll let you be the judge. If you're ready, we can go there now."

Alexandra nodded. Though it was dangerous to her heart, she knew that she would follow Nathan anywhere.

## Chapter Nine

"May I have this dance," Nathan said. The reception was in full swing, and the dance floor was rapidly filling. He had fulfilled his obligation as co-best man. He'd posed for even more pictures once Jillian and Miles entered the ballroom and had danced with the bridesmaid. Isaac had wanted to make the toast and Nathan had agreed. Isaac knew just what to say to amuse the audience all the while making the bride and groom happy. Nathan had never liked having the spotlight shine on him, so he was relieved when his official duties had been completed. Now it was time to party.

"I suppose so," Alexandra said, a smile on her face. He noticed that she smiled easily and often. It was a sincere smile that reflected her inner happiness. And it was quite disarming.

She placed her soft hand into his. He felt a spark of electricity at the contact. He was becoming increasingly attracted to her, so his reaction wasn't unexpected. Nor was it unwanted. Filled with anticipation of holding her in his arms again, he led her to the dance floor. The ballroom was enormous and even with the elaborately decorated tables spaced around the edge and the stage where the band was now playing, there was still plenty of room to dance. The band was playing a ballad and Nathan pulled Alexandra close, then wrapped his arms around her tiny waist.

He'd been looking forward to holding her next to him from the moment she'd opened the door this afternoon and he'd seen her standing there. Dressed in a reddish dress that accentuated every inch of her body, she was quite easily the most beautiful woman he'd ever seen. Even in the sea of jewels and designer dresses, she stood out.

Alexandra's wraparound satin dress was demure, but there was no disguising her sexy body. Over the past few days, he'd tried to convince himself that the rightness he'd felt the last time they danced had been a figment of his imagination. Now, with her soft breasts pressed against his chest, he acknowledged that he hadn't exaggerated things. In fact, he might have undersold his reaction.

They moved together as if they had been dance partners for years as opposed to only one night before. This wasn't something that he did frequently, but he was willing to make an exception tonight. Truthfully, he had made several exceptions since Alexandra had become a part of his life.

That thought shocked him and he stopped dancing. Alexandra stepped back and gave him a questioning look. He got himself together and pulled her against him once more, and they began to sway to the music. Though his body moved in time to the beat, his mind was miles away. One question kept echoing though his brain. Why had he thought that Alexandra had become a part of his life? Sure, the notion held certain appeal—too much appeal for his comfort—but he had his plans, and she didn't fit into them.

He knew rationally that he could make a place for a woman in his life if he wanted to. But women needed time and attention. Two things that he was unable and unwilling to sacrifice. Any time he spent with a woman was time that he couldn't spend working on improving the ranch. Time that would delay implementation of his five-year plan.

Sacrificing his time was fine every once in a while. He did like the occasional break. And he wasn't opposed to a no-strings-attached fling here and there. After all, he wasn't a monk. But anything serious or long-term? That was a nonstarter. So why was he considering making an exception with Alexandra?

Maybe it was the environment. He'd been surrounded by wedding planning for months. All of that talk of love and happily-ever-after had taken its toll on him. Today—with the promises to love and cherish forever and songs about devotion—had been even more of the same. Even a single-minded businessman wasn't immune to the effects of being bombarded by romance nonstop.

But it was more than the perfume scented air, the abundant flowers, and the flowing champagne that was affecting his thinking. It was Alexandra.

Nathan inhaled deeply in an effort to clear his head. Instead he got a whiff of her intoxicating scent and found himself being swept up by his emotions again. Although it was the opposite of clearing his mind, Nathan breathed in again, allowing the scent to completely envelop him.

Nathan could try to resist her appeal, but he knew it was senseless to try to control his reaction. Apparently he was powerless when it came to Alexandra.

"Do you have a nickname?" he asked, blurting the first thing that came to his mind. Anything to stop his mind from traveling down the road it was going. "You know, like a shortened version of Alexandra?"

"Not now. When I was younger, my friends and family called my Lexi."

"*Lexi.* I like that. Why'd you stop using it?"

She shrugged, and he felt her smiling against his shoulder. "I grew up. When I started college, I wanted a more mature-sounding name. Lexi didn't seem professional enough to be a nurse's name. So I became Alexandra."

"I understand."

"What about you? Does anybody call you Nate?"

"Not if they expect me to answer."

She laughed, and he not only heard the sound, he felt it.

The song merged into the next. This one was a line dance, and Nathan reluctantly released Alexandra. He enjoyed the dance, but he much preferred slow dancing, where he would be able to hold her.

When the dance ended, Alexandra grabbed his hand. "I need a break."

"How about we get a drink?"

He turned and nearly ran into Isaac. Naturally his brother would appear at the worst time.

"Hi. I'm Nathan's brother Isaac." He held out his hand to Alexandra, who took it, and then he gestured to the woman standing beside him. "And this is Savannah, my fiancée."

"Nice to meet you both."

"Alexandra and I were just going to get a drink," Nathan said.

"That's a good idea," Isaac said. "But before you do that, you might want to introduce Alexandra to Mom and Dad."

"Right." He should have done that earlier. After all, he'd brought Alexandra with him in order to convince his mother he didn't need her interfering in his love life.

Isaac nodded, then he and Savannah walked away.

When they were alone, Nathan turned to Alexandra. He hoped she wasn't too uncomfortable with the idea.

She grinned and grabbed his arm. "I suppose it's time to put on the show."

"You're okay with this?"

"Of course. This is why you brought me, right?"

"Yes." But he was beginning to believe that wasn't the only reason. And that could be a problem.

Nathan led her over to where his parents sat, smiles on their faces. Nathan quickly made the introductions.

"It's so nice to meet you both," Alexandra said, her look encompassing his parents. "I've heard so many nice things about you."

"It's nice meeting you too," Michelle said. "Won't you sit down so we can talk?"

Nathan smothered a groan.

"They don't want to talk," Edward said. "These young people want to dance. And I would like a few more dances with my best girl too."

"Oh you." Michelle giggled and took the hand Edward held out to her. She glanced at Alexandra and Nathan. "Enjoy the rest of the night."

Nathan kissed his mother's cheek before leading Alexandra away.

"That wasn't too bad," Nathan said.

He introduced her to Miles and Jillian. They got their drinks and then returned to the dance floor. After a few dances, the leader of the band announced that the bride was about to throw the bouquet.

"Yeah, I definitely need to get off the floor," Alexandra said, picking up her pace.

"Oh no. All the single ladies are supposed to try to catch the bouquet. It's tradition."

"I'm not interested in getting married."

"Don't tell me that you believe that catching the bouquet has any type of special powers? Are you the superstitious type? Oooh." He waved his hands as if conjuring up a ghost.

"Not at all."

He leaned closer, teasing her. "Then what's the harm? What if none of the other single ladies get in line? Think about how sad Jillian will feel."

Alexandra shook her head. "You are incorrigible."

"So I've been told."

"I'm going to stand in the back and I'm not going to try to catch it."

"Famous last words."

Alexandra shooed Nathan away and then joined the women assembling in the middle of the dance floor. Although catching the bouquet was supposed to be good fun, it was clear from the way some of the others were boxing out that they were taking it quite seriously. Perhaps they really did believe that catching the bouquet was the first step toward catching the man.

Jillian held up the bouquet and then turned her back to the women who were clustered close together. Alexandra expected Jillian to pretend to throw the floral arrangement in order to amp up the tension, so she was surprised when the flowers went sailing through the air. And landed right in her hands.

There was a smattering of applause and some good-natured groaning as the other women walked away. Jillian and Alexandra posed for a few pictures before Alexandra returned to Nathan's side. He nodded his head toward the bouquet, a wide smile on his face.

"Don't say a word."

"Oh, but I have to. It looks like your plan went awry."

Alexandra shook her head. "I don't know how it happened. One minute I was standing there, way behind everyone, minding my own business."

"And the next?"

She held up the small bouquet, letting the flowers do the talking for her.

Nathan laughed and draped his arm over her shoulder, pulling her next to his side. They fit together so perfectly that for a moment she wished their relationship was real. They got their drinks and found a quiet corner to talk. After two songs, Alexandra set her empty glass on a table and shimmied her shoulders in a clear signal that she wanted to dance.

Alexandra and Nathan danced to just about every song, stopping only to sip some champagne when they got thirsty. By the time the party began to wind down, Alexandra was certain that she had never had a better time in her life. She was actually sorry for the night to come to an end.

She and Nathan recounted the events of the day as he drove her back home. They laughed and talked easily and she was surprised to realize that Nathan was parking in front of Aunt Rose's house.

"Wow. I can't believe we got here so soon," she said, managing to mask her disappointment.

"Time flies when you're having fun," Nathan quipped.

"True. I guess this means our time together has come to an end."

Nathan got out of the car, and Alexandra waited patiently while he circled it and then opened her door for her. She took his hand and let him help her from the car. When he didn't release her hand, she smiled to herself and held on to his.

Her heart began to pound as they climbed the stairs and approached the front door. Memories of the last time they'd said good-night played in her mind. Despite reminding herself that they'd agreed the kiss couldn't ever be repeated, her heart sped up in anticipation of the possibility. Their decision had made sense at the time, since they had no plans of seeing each other again. Now Alexandra wondered why she had ever thought the no-kiss rule was a good idea. Now that she was so close to Nathan that the heat from his body caressed hers, she couldn't imagine not wanting to kiss him. Just the thought of his lips capturing hers made her feel tingly all over.

Surely one little kiss wouldn't hurt anything. They could go back to their previous relationship afterward. The moment the thought crossed her mind, she knew she was lying. It wouldn't be one little kiss. If she had her way, it would be several extremely hot kisses. Heck, she was longing for a live and in color make-out session. If only they hadn't gotten out of the car, they could be necking like teenagers in his back seat. That thought made her laugh out loud.

"What's so funny?" Nathan asked, turning to face each other.

"You won't get it."

"Really? I have a great sense of humor."

"Now that's funny," she said, laughing again.

"You've hurt my feelings."

"I'm sorry." She didn't think he was being serious, but she could be wrong. They were standing in the shadows, so she couldn't see his face. The last thing she wanted to do was offend him. Not simply because she didn't want such a perfect day to end on a sour note, but because she liked him as a person and wouldn't want to hurt him.

"Prove it. Tell me what you found so funny."

"All right," she said. It didn't make sense to hide her feelings from him. And if she was lucky, he'd been thinking the same thing. A girl could hope. She took a deep breath and then blurted out, "I was thinking that we should have stayed in the car so we could make out."

He huffed out a laugh that did little to mask his surprise. "Wow. You just put it out there."

She shrugged. "You asked."

"That I did." He paused for several long seconds and suddenly she felt anxious. Maybe honesty wasn't always the best policy.

"You can always forget I said anything."

"Why would I want to do that?" He reached out slowly, and she held her breath as she waited for his hand to caress her cheek. His touch was gentle. Sweet. Of their own volition, her eyes floated shut, and she leaned into his palm. He brushed his callused thumb over her lips and desire pooled in her stomach.

She forced her eyes open and looked at him. His eyes were dark with longing that made hers even stronger. "So what are we going to do?"

He moved even closer. So close that she could feel his heart beating. "What's the worst that could happen if we kiss? You know, one more for the road?"

"I can't think of even one negative thing," she whispered.

"Then let's go for it," he murmured, a second before his lips captured hers in a searing kiss that took her breath away. They'd kissed before, and the memory of that kiss had been etched in her mind. But compared to this one, that one had been a peck. She opened her mouth to him and his tongue swept inside. Moaning her pleasure, her tongue tangled and danced with his. Hungry for more, she pressed closer, molding her body against his.

She had no idea how much time passed, but when he began to pull away, gradually ending the kiss, she was gasping for breath. Slowly she became aware of her surroundings. They were standing on her aunt's porch. She straightened her dress and then leaned against his chest. His breath was labored, and she felt his chest rise and fall beneath her forehead.

After she'd regained her composure, she leaned back and glanced into his face. His eyes were just as intense as before. Maybe more so. Needing to lighten the mood and diminish the sexual attraction crackling between them, she smiled. "I knew we should have stayed in the car."

A startled expression crossed his face a moment before he barked out a laugh. "Making out in the car would definitely be a new one for me."

"Really?" She allowed her voice to reflect the skepticism she felt. He might be the serious "all work and no play" type now, but she didn't for a moment believe he'd always been that way. After all, he'd been a teenage boy with raging hormones once. She couldn't believe the girls in town hadn't been all over him back then. "I find that hard to believe."

"Perhaps I should have said since I reached adulthood."

"That sounds more believable if a little bit…"

"A little bit what? Boring?"

"Sad. Even at our age we should experience the joy—and terror of being discovered—of necking in the back seat of a car."

He laughed. "I'll keep that in mind."

She eased back, slowly increasing the distance between them. When no part of her body enjoyed the pleasure of touching his, she sighed. "I suppose we need to say good-night now."

"Yes. I really enjoyed spending time with you. Maybe we can do it again sometime."

"I'm willing whenever you are." Alexandra realized that saying that made her sound desperate, but it was too late to call the words back. Besides, she'd only spoken the truth. She would enjoy spending more time with Nathan. They were both clear about where they stood, so neither of them would have to worry about getting a broken heart.

What more could they ask for?

## Chapter Ten

"So, you and Alexandra?"

Nathan turned to look at his brother. Isaac was leaning against the fence, an exceedingly annoying expression on his face. Since Miles was honeymooning in Fiji, Nathan would be stuck dealing with Isaac on his own for the next ten days. Although he had matured a lot since Mia and Savannah had come into his life, his core personality hadn't changed. He still possessed that pesky little brother attitude that Nathan expected him to have at ninety.

"I brought her to the wedding Saturday. You saw her."

"And I noticed the way that you wouldn't let anyone else near her all night. I barely had the chance to say two words to her."

"That's not true. She was free to interact with whomever she chose."

"But when the real party started—you know dancing and talking—you were glued to her side. She might not have noticed, but I saw the way you mean mugged every man who even looked like he might come over to talk to her or ask her to dance."

Nathan couldn't deny that. But he wasn't going to admit it either. His time with Alexandra had been limited, and he hadn't wanted to share her with anyone. "She was my date, so I was responsible for her. She's new to town. She doesn't know which guys are serious and which ones would try to take advantage of her."

"So you were doing your civic duty?" Isaac laughed. "How big of you. We both know that every guy there was a stand-up type. Or they wouldn't have been invited."

Of course he knew that. But he'd felt strangely protective of her. More than that, he'd felt possessive, which was ridiculous. She didn't belong to him. They weren't involved romantically. Besides, he didn't believe that a person could own another. People stayed in relationships because they wanted to. That is the only way it could work.

"Did you want something?"

Isaac's grin spread slowly. "Just to tell you that I like Alexandra and to invite the two of you to have dinner with me and Savannah."

Nathan hooked the heel of his boot through the fence and thought for a second. He liked Savannah. She was the perfect woman for his brother. He enjoyed her company and thought Alexandra would too.

Going to dinner could be fun. It would also be

a good way to keep his mother off his back. They hadn't had Sunday dinner this past week, and Nathan had been looking forward to having a reprieve. It hadn't come. His mother had called him before noon Sunday. She'd grilled him about Alexandra for so long he was surprised he didn't have sear lines on his body.

After seeing them together at the wedding, his mother had decided that they belonged together. Now Michelle would stop trying to set him up with a friend's cousin's next-door neighbor. Mission accomplished. But he might have succeeded too well, because now his mother had zeroed in on Alexandra. He could tell that she was already planning their future. She'd dropped hints about him bringing Alexandra around so she could get to know her better.

Although Alexandra had agreed to go to the wedding with him as part of the charade, he wasn't sure she would be amenable to carrying it on endlessly. After all, she'd been clear that she wasn't interested in a relationship. That's why he'd invited her to the wedding. She was a safe date who wouldn't be interested in trying to become a part of his life. If he asked her to continue the pretense for a while longer, she might think he was trying to intrude on hers.

He thought he'd been clever. Now it looked like he had outsmarted himself. If he told his mother that he and Alexandra weren't dating, she would start setting him up again. He didn't want to live through that. Just the thought was enough to make him break out in hives.

There was only one thing to do. He needed to convince Alexandra to extend their pretend relationship. She'd been so leery when he'd mentioned the charade and he'd been afraid she wouldn't go along with his plan. But since it was only make-believe, she'd gone along with it.

But the pretend relationship was starting to feel like a real one. That was a problem. Neither of them wanted anything that was remotely like a commitment. If he made too many demands on her time, she might back out. This was going to take a masterful negotiation.

"Let me get in touch with Alexandra and get back to you."

"Whoa. That is totally unexpected. I thought we had moved past that part of the conversation."

"We can. If your invitation wasn't sincere, that's fine."

Isaac laughed and raised his hands. "Oh no you don't, Nathan. You aren't going to weasel out that easily. Talk to Alexandra and get back to me."

"I'll let you know." He pushed away from the fence and headed for his horse. "Let's get back to work. Time's a wasting."

As they worked, Nathan's mind kept wandering to Alexandra and the last time he'd seen her. She'd been so radiant and full of life. Just being around her had made his heart beat faster. Thinking that she wouldn't be a part of his life had left him feeling empty. Bereft even, something he hadn't expected.

He hadn't wanted their time to come to an end, but he'd known that they couldn't pursue a relationship. So there was no reason for them to keep seeing each other.

Now he could spend time with her without having the expectations that accompanied a relationship. That is, if he could get her to agree. Alexandra's reluctance to date had just as much to do with time constraints as it did with an unwillingness to risk heartbreak. Although he could promise that her heart would be safe—he didn't want her love and wasn't giving his—a fake relationship could take just as much time as a real one.

Somehow, he would have to persuade her that he wouldn't take up too much of her time. Now that he had a reason to talk to Alexandra again, he couldn't wait for the workday to end so he could phone her. Just the thought of hearing her sultry voice sent blood pulsing through his veins. So naturally, they kept finding holes in the fence, and repairing them made the day drag on. He was relieved by the time they'd finished, and he stepped into his house.

After a quick shower followed by an equally quick dinner, Nathan grabbed his phone and dialed Alexandra's number. His heart sped up as the phone rang and he took a deep breath. He didn't want to sound like a teenager whose voice was changing, squeaking whenever he talked to a girl that he had a crush on.

The call went to voice mail. Disappointed, he left

a message. The depth of his disappointment gave him pause. Perhaps it was a good thing that she didn't answer. He didn't want to get too attached to her. Maybe he needed to take a step back and rethink this plan.

"What are you doing here?" Lynn, one of the night shift nurses, asked Alexandra on Tuesday night as she came into the locker room. "Isn't this your day off?"

"It was," Alexandra said, turning to look at her friend and coworker. "Carla had an emergency and needed to switch schedules, so I came in for her."

"Is she still having trouble with her ex?"

"Sadly, yes," Alexandra said. Although she was disappointed that Chloe wouldn't have a father in her life, she was relieved not to have this kind of drama. Alexandra reached into her locker and took out a bag. "I didn't have plans. But now my shift is over. I have one thing to do, and then I'm going home."

"What's in the bag?" Lynn asked, draping her stethoscope over her neck.

"It's something for Emma. I'm still trying to lift her spirits."

"That's nice. I hope it works. I'm fresh out of ideas."

Emma was a seven-year-old who'd been injured in a car accident. The little girl hadn't been responding to treatment. Worse, she showed little interest in trying and refused to cooperate. "I'll let you know how it works."

Alexandra closed her locker, slapped a red hat on her head, picked up the bag and then headed to Emma's room. The girl's mother, Robin, glanced up when

Alexandra stepped inside. The worried expression on her face morphed into one of confusion.

"Ho, ho, ho," Alexandra said loudly. "Merry Christmas."

Emma had been staring listlessly out the window. Now she turned to look at Alexandra. "It's not Christmastime."

"It's not?" Alexandra said, doing her best to sound perplexed. "Are you sure?"

Emma giggled. "Yes. Christmas is in December. That is not now."

"Oh no. How embarrassing. And I have on this hat." Alexandra pointed to the red elf hat on her head. "I suppose I should take it off."

Emma nodded. "Yes."

Alexandra removed the hat and set it on the empty table. "What am I going to do with this?"

"With what?" Emma pushed herself into a sitting position.

Alexandra pulled a gaily wrapped box from the bag and held it up. "It has your name on it. Do you suppose Santa got confused too?"

"Can that happen?" Emma asked, looking at her mother.

"Maybe," Robin said.

"I should probably give it to you," Alexandra said. "I don't want Santa to get angry with us."

Emma's arm and hand had been injured and she hadn't been participating in her therapy. Now she reached out for the box. Alexandra stepped up to the bed and handed over the package.

Emma placed it on her lap. "I wonder what it is."

"Open it and see," Alexandra urged.

Emma's mother reached out to help her, and Alexandra shook her head *no.*

Alexandra had worked with Emma's physical therapist, who'd wrapped the box. Now Alexandra watched as the little girl struggled. It took some effort, but eventually she managed to remove the paper and tape.

"A doll! It's a doll." Emma turned the box so her mother could look. "It's a new doll."

"Wow. That's wonderful."

"I want to play with her."

"That sounds like a good plan," Alexandra said. "What are you going to name her?"

"Jenna. That's my sister's name."

"And it's a good one."

Alexandra hung out for a few more minutes, watching as Emma played with the doll. She was livelier than she'd been since she'd come to the hospital and was actually using her hands as much as she could.

Satisfied that the little girl was on the mend, Alexandra picked up the hat. "Well, I need to get going. Have fun with your doll."

Emma nodded. "Bye."

"Thank you so much," Robin said.

"You're welcome. Good night."

Alexandra was tired but happy as she headed home. She checked in on Chloe, grateful that her little girl was safe and healthy. Then she took a quick shower and pulled on a pair of her comfiest pajamas. While she ate dinner, she checked her messages. When she heard Nathan's voice, her heart skipped a beat.

She debated about whether it was too late to call and then decided to take a chance. "Is it a good time?" she asked instead of saying hello.

"It is the best time."

His answer made her smile. "Sorry I missed your call. I switched days with a friend."

"Are you tired?"

"No. I took a shower and now I've got my second wind."

"Great." She heard him inhale and then blow it out. "I was wondering if you are free to talk."

"Of course. We're talking now."

"Actually, I was hoping we could talk in person."

"That sounds ominous." She managed to keep her sudden stress from her voice.

"It's not. Everything is fine."

"Okay. Then come on over."

"Great. I'm on my way. I'll be there in a little while."

Alexandra ended the call and changed into a pair of faded jeans, a purple top and purple socks. She pulled a comb through her hair and then added a purple floral headband to hold it away from her face.

Her mind raced wildly as she waited impatiently for Nathan to arrive. Was he going to tell her that their friendship was over? If so, why would he do that in person? And why was that such a big deal?

Fortunately, the doorbell rang before her mind could travel too far down that road, and she walked to the door.

"Come on in," she said, softly. She held out her arm, gesturing for him to precede her into the living room. "Would you like something to eat or drink?"

Nathan shook his head and sat on the sofa where she'd indicated and looked around the room. With high ceilings, crown molding, and comfortable old furniture, the room was charming and cozy. He took a deep breath and forced himself to relax. "Maybe in a little while. But you go ahead if you want something."

"I have my cocoa." She picked up a mug and then took a swallow. "I love hot cocoa. I can't get enough of the stuff."

He couldn't get enough of watching the way her tongue darted out and dabbed at the tiniest bit of chocolate at the corner of her mouth. It was so erotic that he began to sweat. Perhaps he should have taken her up on her offer. He could use a cold drink right about now.

She leaned back against the chair and then crossed her ankles. She looked relaxed and he found himself relaxing too. It was amazing how at ease he felt with her. It felt completely natural to unwind with her at the end of the day.

"So, what did you want to talk about?"

He was glad to get right to the point. "I have a proposal for you."

She pressed her hands against her chest, smiled, and batted her eyes. "This is so sudden. I thought we were just friends." His breath stalled. Before he could say anything, she burst out laughing. "Sorry. I couldn't resist. Breathe before you pass out."

He inhaled. "You really are funny."

She grinned, clearly still amused. "You just looked so shocked. Then you looked like you might keel over at any minute. You know I was just teasing, right? We agreed that neither of us wants a relationship."

"I know we said that. But maybe I could change your mind."

Her eyes widened. "About having a relationship? Are you serious?"

Now it was his turn to laugh. "No. I was thinking about the wedding. We convinced a lot of people that we were a couple."

She nodded slowly, clearly wary.

"We could keep a lot of people off my back if we pretended for a while longer."

"By people, you mean your mother?"

He nodded. "As long as my mother thinks that we're involved, I won't have to worry about a strange woman showing up at Sunday dinner."

She looked a bit skeptical. "And you believe you can avoid this if I pretend to be your girlfriend."

He heard the confusion in her voice and was instantly reminded that he'd thought the idea was ludicrous. But it was out there now. "Yes. That's the plan."

"I don't know, Nathan. It sounds complicated."

"It isn't."

"Sure it is. It's not as if your mother is the only person in town. Other people will see us as well. Eventually our friends and my coworkers will hear about our supposed relationship. That's a complication if I ever heard of one. And that's just the beginning."

"Are you worried about a potential boyfriend hearing that you're involved?" He didn't know why the thought of Alexandra being with another man irritated him, but it did.

"Not even a little bit. I have no plans of seeing another man. A relationship is the last thing that I want."

The relief he felt was outsized. And disturbing. This pretend relationship shouldn't matter that much to him. If Alexandra decided she wanted to have a real relationship in the future, that was her right. It had nothing to do with him.

"Then why do you think this will be complicated?"

"Because. You can't just tell your mother that we're dating and have that be the end of it. You live on the same ranch. If you go about your regular routine, she'll know. In order for this to work, she has to see us together. That means we have to spend time together."

"I know. Is that going to be a problem?"

Alexandra inhaled deeply before answering. It didn't take a genius to know that this was not going to be as simple as Nathan believed. Things like this never were. Pretending to date would be playing with fire. No matter how hard they tried to ignore the simmering attraction between them, it was real. The kisses they'd shared were the hottest of her life. Pretending to be involved romantically could lead to complications. Even knowing that she could get burned, she was hard-pressed to think of kissing Nathan as a negative.

Alexandra realized that Nathan was still waiting for her response. Before she could give him an answer, she needed more details. "How long would this last?"

"I don't know. I guess until we convince my mother that we're serious. She needs to believe that I'm willing to have more to my life than the ranch. Once she's convinced, we can stage a breakup."

"I don't know. I don't need that kind of drama. Are you sure there isn't some other reason you want to do this?"

He smirked. "You know, I am quite the catch."

She laughed. "I don't doubt it."

"I suppose having a girlfriend could help with business. Occasionally I have business dinners and a date would help."

She nodded. "I can do social events. At least on some weekends with enough notice."

"This goes both ways. I'm willing to be your pretend boyfriend whenever you need one."

"I'm not expecting to need one, but thanks for the offer."

He rose, paced to the window and back. Then he sat on the edge of the couch. She'd never seen him so nervous. Obviously this meant a lot to him. "So... will you do it?"

Alexandra knew she should say no, but she couldn't do him like that. He was kind and generous and he needed this favor. And to be honest, she liked spending time with Nathan and wouldn't mind seeing him more often. She was just afraid of getting hurt.

But this plan could be the best of both worlds. She could spend time with Nathan—enjoying his quick wit—and hopefully his hot kisses—without risking her heart.

"Well," Nathan prompted when she didn't respond.

She sucked in a breath. If she agreed, there would be no turning back. But then, she wouldn't want to. "I'm in. I'll be your pretend girlfriend for as long as you need."

His brilliant smile set butterflies free in her stomach, and she felt tingly all over. "Now we need to put our plan into action."

"How about now?" She flashed him a saucy grin. "Do we need to synchronize our watches like they did in old movies?"

He chuckled. "I think we can skip that. When are you available to date?"

"My social life is limited to girls' night out every couple of weeks, so other than work, I'm free most of the time. Of course, I have a child who needs a lot of my attention."

"I don't want to take away your time with your daughter. In fact, if you're okay with me being around your daughter, I don't see a reason why she can't be a part of our dates."

"Really?"

"Yes. If we were dating for real, I would want to have a relationship with her. As much as you would allow."

Tears suddenly pricked her eyes and Alexandra blinked them away. She hoped Nathan hadn't noticed.

She knew that Nathan was kind, but she was still caught unaware by how considerate he was. Owen hadn't been interested in Chloe, so Nathan's willingness to welcome her daughter into his life was especially touching.

"I think that would be nice."

"Great." He paused and inhaled. When he spoke again, his voice was husky. "I don't have kids, and my experience is limited to my nieces and nephew. But you can trust me. Chloe will always be safe with me."

"I appreciate you saying that. But you don't have to worry about being alone with Chloe. Since we're only pretend dating, we'll always be together."

Chloe was one of the reasons that Alexandra didn't want to get involved with a man. She didn't want her little girl to become attached to someone who might not stay in her life. Alexandra would rather be alone than break her daughter's heart. She knew letting her daughter get close to Nathan was risky. But in this instance, she believed the benefit of having another person around to love her was worth the risk. After all, she didn't want her daughter to become afraid to love.

Besides, Alexandra didn't expect their fake relationship to last long enough for Chloe to become attached to Nathan. A few dates here and there should be enough to convince Nathan's mother that he had more in his life than work.

"I also know that you're worried about letting Chloe get too close to me. You don't have to be. No matter what, I'll always take care of your little girl. Her heart will be safe with me."

Alexandra's vision blurred and she blinked. This pretend relationship was becoming more emotional than she'd anticipated. It was time to get back to the purely pragmatic issues.

"We should do something together soon," Alexandra said. Just saying the words made her heart pound and for a brief moment she second-guessed her decision to agree to this plan. One thing was certain, she and Nathan couldn't kiss again. Alexandra might have a lot of willpower, but it took more than willpower to control her heart. It would be too easy to fall for Nathan.

"What do you have in mind?"

"I had a great time visiting the ranch. I think Chloe would enjoy seeing the horses. That is, if you think that it's safe." And Chloe's presence would keep them from possibly becoming too affectionate.

"Remember, I grew up on the ranch. I was sitting on a horse in front of my father when I was younger than she is. My nieces and nephew have already been on horses with my brothers."

"Are you saying that you want to put Chloe on a horse?" Alexandra couldn't disguise her shock.

"Yes. Unless you're opposed to the idea."

"I've never been on a horse, so I certainly don't think that I can comfortably hold her."

He laughed, and the robust sound sent shivers down her spine.

Oh, she was walking a line here. It would be so easy to fall for him.

"I wasn't going to suggest that. If you're okay with it, I'll hold her on the horse with me."

"I think she might like it."

"And what about you? Would you like it?"

"Riding on a horse with you?" The image his words created in her mind was quite enticing. She could imagine how good it would feel to sit in front of him and lean back against his strong chest. How wonderful it would feel to be close enough to inhale his masculine scent while the heat from his body kept hers warm.

"That's not what I meant, but now that you mention it…" His voice lowered seductively, and his eyes appeared even darker.

Alexandra swallowed before answering. Even then, her voice was barely louder than a whisper. "I think that I can ride on my own. And I would love seeing Chloe on a horse in front of you."

"Then how about Saturday?"

"That works for me."

"Then it's a date."

## Chapter Eleven

Alexandra set Chloe onto the floor before she ran to open the door. They were going to visit the Montgomery ranch today. Although Alexandra was perfectly capable of driving and had offered to do so, Nathan had insisted on picking them up. This is what he'd do if they were dating for real. According to him, they would never fool his mother if he acted out of character.

Dressed in a blue plaid shirt that emphasized his muscular torso and faded jeans, Nathan looked like he'd stepped out of a men's magazine. He smiled, and her heart nearly burst from her chest. It was so sweet and tender that she could almost believe that he was truly interested in her.

Shaking her head at such a foolish thought, she smiled back. "Welcome. Thank you so much for coming to pick us up."

"It is a date," he said, as if that explained everything. And to him it did.

"I suppose it is."

"And if this was a real date, I would do this too." Before she could guess his intent, he leaned over and brushed a kiss against her cheek. His gentle touch was devastating. Electricity shot through her body and her temperature rose at least five degrees. He pulled back and then looked at her, a twinkle in his eyes. "I hope that was okay to do."

"If we are going to make this look real, we need to stay in character at all times."

He smiled and nodded. Alexandra had no idea what it would be like to date Nathan, but if this was an example of how he treated a woman, it must be wonderful.

Alexandra led him into the front room. Chloe was standing, using the coffee table to keep her balance. She looked up and flashed a snaggletoothed grin. Alexandra scooped her up and then turned so that her little girl could get a look at Nathan.

She believed that you could tell a lot about a person by how they treated children. Nathan leaned over and smiled at Chloe. "Hello, Chloe. My name is Nathan."

Chloe grinned and then leaned her face into Alexandra's breast. After a moment, she turned her head and peeked at Nathan. Alexandra had a busy life and frequently took Chloe with her when she ran errands, so her daughter had been around many people. It was rare for her to be shy, so Alexandra wasn't sure what to make of her daughter's behavior. After a few seconds,

Chloe lifted her head, looked at Nathan, and babbled a few syllables at him.

"Is that right?" Nathan asked.

Chloe nodded and chattered some more.

Alexandra watched with pleasure as Nathan and Chloe interacted. After a moment, Nathan stood to his full height, then took a good look at Alexandra and Chloe. He grinned. "You two look so cute."

*Cute* wasn't what Alexandra had been going for, at least for herself, but she tried not to feel disappointed by his comment. After all, he wasn't her real boyfriend. She'd been feeling a little bit frivolous today, so she'd dressed herself and Chloe in the same color. They were each wearing orange tops and blue jeans. Alexandra had found a cute pair of cowboy boots and a cowboy hat for Chloe.

"Thanks. I thought this would work in case we took pictures."

"Oh, we're definitely taking a few pictures to memorialize the day. Especially since this is Chloe's first time on a horse."

"Well then, let's get this day started."

Alexandra nodded and the trio left on their adventure.

Nathan removed the car seat from Alexandra's car and then secured it in the back seat of his car. Once Chloe was settled in her seat, Alexandra and Nathan got inside. Nathan started the car and then paired his phone to the car's sound system. Children's music began to play through the speaker.

Alexandra glanced at Nathan. "This is a surprise."

"I told you, I have a kids' playlist. My nieces and nephew like listening to it, so I figured Chloe would too."

Apparently Nathan's thoughtfulness was limitless. "She is starting to appreciate music. This is one of her favorite songs."

Chloe was too young to sing, but she made happy sounds and clapped.

Nathan flashed her a wicked grin before turning his attention back to the road. "Quiet as it's kept, a few of these songs are starting to grow on me. I've caught myself singing one every once in a while."

"A couple of them are quite catchy."

"It was a bit unsettling to find myself singing about being a pizza and a family of sharks at first but now I just go with it."

Alexandra laughed. "It takes a big man to admit that he likes kids' songs."

"Hold on a minute. I didn't say I liked listening to them. I just said that they pop into my mind and out of my mouth at the strangest time."

"Well, I'm glad we got that straight," Alexandra teased. "I would hate to ruin your reputation as a serious rancher and hard businessman."

"Is that my reputation?"

"You don't know?"

He shrugged. "It's hard to know what others think about you. It's generally not something they discuss with you."

"True. Does having that reputation bother you?"

"I don't see why it should. I am focused on running the ranch."

"Is that enough for you?"

"It is for now."

She nodded. She knew that was true. He wouldn't need her to pretend to be his girlfriend otherwise. He would have a real one. One day, after he'd accomplished his business goals, he would find a woman to love for real and stop pretending.

That was one more reason why Alexandra couldn't allow herself to forget that this relationship was only make-believe.

Nathan turned onto the road leading to the ranch and then drove straight to his house. After he parked, Alexandra got out of the car and then helped Chloe from the car seat. As he watched the mother and daughter duo, he felt a strange stirring near his heart. There was something about being around the two of them that filled him with a sense of peace. Not that peace was lacking in his life. It wasn't.

He didn't want to waste time pondering his feelings and trying to figure them out. He had a full day of fun planned. Before they headed for the stables, he wanted to drop the baby gear in the house. He grabbed up the assorted paraphernalia that babies needed and then led the way up the stairs.

They stepped inside and he dropped Chloe's play mat and bag of toys beside the front door. Though Alexandra had only been to his house once, it felt as if she belonged here.

"Would you like something to eat? Drink?"

Alexandra shook her head. "No."

"In that case, we should take Chloe out to see the horses."

Alexandra smiled brightly and his stomach did a ridiculous flip-flop. "I'm looking forward to seeing them too. And the cows. I had such a good time before. I couldn't stop thinking about it."

"Why didn't you say something? I told you that you could come back anytime. I meant it."

The look on her face nearly broke his heart as he realized that she hadn't believed he'd meant it when he said she was always welcome. He wondered how many times she had been disappointed by someone who'd broken a promise to her. Chloe's father would have to be at the top of the list.

What kind of man deceived a woman as sweet as Alexandra then abandoned his own child? How could a man live with himself when he had no idea if his child—his own flesh and blood—was safe and warm? How could he function without knowing if that child had enough to eat?

"Is something wrong?" Alexandra asked. Her soft voice was troubled, and her normally smooth brow was wrinkled.

No doubt his unpleasant thoughts were written all over his face. He forced his disgust for the other man away and smiled. He didn't want to waste time with Alexandra thinking about someone who wasn't worth it. "Not at all. Everything is perfect. Whenever you're ready, we can go to the stable."

"I'm ready now." Alexandra picked up her daughter and looked at her. "Do you want to see a horsey?"

Chloe babbled and grabbed a fistful of Alexandra's hair and gave it a tug. Alexandra winced and tried to work her hair free.

"Do you need some help?" Nathan asked, even though he was unsure what good he could do.

At the sound of his voice, Chloe turned in his direction, pulling Alexandra's hair even harder.

"Yes," Alexandra said.

In a flash, Nathan was at her side. He leaned over and tried to free Alexandra's hair. He didn't want to hurt Chloe by being too rough, but he didn't like seeing Alexandra in pain. How could he help one without hurting the other? "What should I do?"

He realized that asking the question probably made him look foolish. Truth be told, he did suddenly feel incompetent. Not at all like the man with the plan.

"If you could hold Chloe, I can work my hair free from her fingers."

"That I can do." He reached out and took the little girl into his arms. He held her gingerly, careful not to squeeze her too tight. "Come here for a minute, Chloe."

The baby gave him a long look and then settled into his chest. She didn't loosen her grip on Alexandra's hair, so Alexandra had no choice but to come along. Nathan inhaled and got a whiff of her perfume. It was light and sexy. Tantalizing. His mind was immediately filled with erotic images, and it took immense effort to force them away. He was supposed to be helping Alexandra, not fantasizing about kissing her senseless and then making love to her until they were both weak.

Once he had Chloe firmly in his arms, Alexandra reached up and began to free her hair from her daughter's hand. She opened the little fingers one by one and then pulled her thick hair away. Chloe laughed and then clapped her chubby hands in pleasure, oblivious to the pain that she'd caused her mother.

Alexandra stood to her full height, which was several inches shorter than his. Her body might be small, but the impact it had on his was enormous. The heat from her body reached out and wrapped around him, pulling him nearer to her. Like a moth drawn to a flame, he was powerless to resist. Their eyes met and he froze, unable to do anything other than stare into hers. Her eyes were a rich brown, and suddenly they were filled with unmistakable longing. The urge to kiss her was strong. Before he could move closer to her, he felt a hard slap on his face.

He jerked.

"No, Chloe. No hitting," Alexandra said. "I'm so sorry."

Nathan just laughed. Perhaps Chloe had been able to read his mind and hadn't approved of the thoughts he was having about her mother. "Don't worry about it."

Alexandra stepped away, then gathered her gorgeous hair into a messy ponytail on top of her head. A pang hit him as he realized just how much he'd liked seeing her hair float free around her face and shoulders, shifting as she moved. But then, it appealed to Chloe too. No doubt she would grab a fistful the first opportunity that she got.

Nathan nodded toward Alexandra's hair. "Does she pull it often?"

"Yes. She's a regular Ms. Grabby Hands. That's why I no longer wear earrings or necklaces around her. I took a chance and left my hair down today. I was trying to be cute. Clearly that was a mistake I won't make again soon."

"You're just as beautiful either way," he blurted out before he could think the better of it. It seemed like the right thing to say. Something a real boyfriend would say. But would a fake boyfriend compliment her appearance when there was no one else around to hear him? No one else over the age of one, that is.

"Thank you." Her voice was barely above a whisper. Her surprised yet gentle smile swept away all of his concerns. Nathan didn't know how many people commented on her appearance these days. In his mind, she was worthy of compliments every day. She was the most beautiful woman he'd ever laid eyes on. Though she was physically stunning, she was equally as beautiful on the inside.

They stood beside each other, silently assessing the other for a moment. When he realized that he was becoming hypnotized by her, he blinked and stepped back, creating a safe distance between them. Her nearness was wreaking havoc with his mind, affecting him in ways he hadn't anticipated. "Come on. Let's go see the horses."

She nodded and reached out for her daughter. "I can take Chloe if you want."

"That's not necessary. She doesn't weigh a thing. Besides, I think that she likes me. Don't you, sweetie?"

Chloe smiled and then leaned her head against his chest. This little one was quickly stealing his heart.

When they stepped outside, he set Chloe on his shoulders, something his nieces and nephew loved. There was something about being high enough to see everything that appealed to the little ones whose view was generally more limited. As expected, Chloe chortled gleefully and kicked her heels against his chest.

He was wearing a cowboy hat, so she wasn't able to grab his hair. Not that it was as long as Alexandra's.

"Is she okay?" Alexandra asked.

He heard the concern in her voice and smiled at her. "I won't let her fall. I have her by the heels with one hand and my other is behind her back. She's perfectly safe."

"I know. I guess it's the mother in me."

"I can set her down if that would make you more comfortable."

She glanced at her daughter, who was babbling and having the time of her life. "No. I trust you."

Those three little words pierced his chest and touched a place in his heart that he hadn't known existed. He didn't know why Alexandra's trust meant so much to him, but it did. Perhaps it was knowing that someone had broken her trust along with her heart. He didn't know.

He was determined to prove himself worthy of that trust.

## Chapter Twelve

Alexandra ordered herself to calm down as she walked beside Nathan in the stable. Her heart had started to race the moment that he helped her free her hair from Chloe's strong little fingers, and it hadn't slowed yet. He'd been standing so close that if she had moved even one centimeter in his direction, they would have been touching. For one blissful moment, she'd thought he might kiss her. Thought she would let him. Thankfully Chloe had broken the moment before Alexandra did something stupid that she would regret.

Nathan wasn't her real boyfriend. She didn't know why she was having such a hard time remembering that and behaving accordingly. It was easy to remember when he was far away from her. It was only a problem when he was near—like when their eyes had met and she'd been captured by his gaze. There was no way around it. Nathan Montgomery was the stuff that fantasies were made of.

Life wasn't a fantasy. There were no fairy god-mothers waving magic wands and turning pumpkins into carriages.

Alexandra looked over at Nathan. He was laughing up at Chloe who was clearly thrilled to be sitting on his broad shoulders. The sight made Alexandra's heart ache for all that her little girl was missing by not having her father in her life. Alexandra knew that lots of children were being raised in single-parent homes and that they were happy. There was no reason Chloe wouldn't thrive as long as she had Alexandra's support.

The expression on Nathan's face as he looked at Chloe touched Alexandra's heart. Clearly it was important to him that Chloe enjoyed herself.

A horse neighed. Chloe let out an excited squeal and craned her neck, trying to find the animal. She twisted on Nathan's shoulders and Alexandra's breath caught in her throat. Before she could gasp, Nathan had swung Chloe around and was now holding her against his chest. Her back was against his body so she could look at the animals without having to turn around. Chloe stretched out her arms, trying to touch the massive animal.

"It looks like she's a fan of horses."

"Looks like," Alexandra agreed.

"If you hold her for a minute, I'll saddle a couple for us. I figure a short ride around the corral will be just right for this little one."

Nathan turned and closed the distance between them. Alexandra admired his wide shoulders and muscular chest. When she realized she was staring, her cheeks got hot, and she glanced away. Once again she reminded herself that their relationship was only pretend. Not only were they not dating now, they wouldn't be dating in the future. Even so, she couldn't stop her heart from pounding as he came near. Nor could she prevent the tingles that skipped up and down her spine when their hands brushed.

He took care to place Chloe in Alexandra's arms and made sure that Alexandra had a secure hold on the baby before stepping away.

Alexandra watched as he walked away, noting that he looked just as good from behind as he did from the front. They might only be pretending to be involved, but her body was feeling the attraction for real.

Nathan moved quickly and efficiently as he put a blanket on the back of each horse, followed quickly by a saddle. Once he'd tightened everything, he grabbed the reins and led the animals through a wide door and into the corral. He looked over his shoulder and smiled at Alexandra. Her heart leaped in reply.

"Come on out here."

Chloe babbled a reply as if speaking for herself as well as Alexandra.

"Coming," Alexandra replied, walking into the corral. The dirt was packed and felt secure under her feet. Even so, she was glad she'd worn her cowboy boots.

When Alexandra reached Nathan, she smiled at him. "How are we going to do this?"

"Let me show you how to mount the horse. You can practice getting on and off. Once you're sure that you can get on by yourself, you can hold Chloe while I get on Excalibur's back. Then I'll hold her while you get on Snowflake. How does that sound?"

"It sounds like a plan." If she could pull it off.

Alexandra held Chloe while Nathan demonstrated how to get on the horse's back. He moved smoothly. Skillfully. The confidence that he demonstrated was proof that he'd done this thousands of times over the year. And it was a complete turn-on.

He swung off the horse's back and stood beside Alexandra. He took Chloe and then smiled. "Now you try. Put your left foot into the stirrup and then swing your right leg over Snowflake's back. I'll be right here in case you need assistance."

Alexandra inhaled a deep breath and then put her foot into the stirrup as Nathan had instructed. She grabbed the reins and then swung her right leg over the horse. When she was sitting in the saddle, she looked around and *whoa*. She was up high. The horse moved beneath her, and she gasped. Then Snowflake stilled. Alexandra smiled. It wasn't that bad. Actually it wasn't bad at all. She kind of liked it. Chloe must have felt the same way when she'd been on Nathan's shoulders.

She slid off the way that she'd watched Nathan dismount.

"Well?" he asked.

"Piece of cake."

"I thought you'd feel that way. You're a natural."

With that, he handed over Chloe and then swung up on Excalibur's back. His horse was positively enormous, but Nathan was totally at ease on it. He held the reins in one hand and then leaned over for Chloe. Alexandra lifted up her child and watched with a bit of trepidation as he took her daughter into his arms and settled her on the saddle in front of him. Chloe giggled and wiggled her whole body in excitement.

"Well, we don't have to wonder if she likes horses. She's definitely a ranch child at heart," Nathan said.

"Apparently." Alexandra started to get on Snowflake's back. At the last minute, she pulled out her phone and snapped a few pictures of Chloe and Nathan on Excalibur's back for posterity's sake. Then she slid her phone back into her pocket so she could mount the horse. Alexandra mentally reviewed Nathan's directions, then swung up into Snowflake's saddle. The horse took a step or two and then stilled.

"You did that like a pro," Nathan said. "Nobody could tell me you haven't been riding for years."

Alexandra winked. "I had a great teacher."

"How about we walk around the corral?" Nathan suggested.

"Sounds good. Besides, I don't think Chloe will be happy with just being on the horse's back. She knows that she is supposed to go somewhere."

Nathan gave Excalibur the signal to move, and the horse began to walk slowly around the corral. Alexandra gave Snowflake a gentle kick, and she began to follow Excalibur. Although Chloe hadn't yet mas-

tered the art of talking, she was perfectly capable of
expressing her feelings.

Alexandra urged her horse to go faster so that she
and Nathan were riding side by side. As expected,
Chloe was smiling brightly as she enjoyed this new
experience. But it was Nathan's expression that held
her attention. She'd never seen him as relaxed as he
was now in his natural element.

Then he glanced down at Chloe, and Alexandra's
breath caught in her throat. It was a look she'd seen
many times on her own father's face whenever he
looked at one of his children. It was a look of pure
pride.

That thought brought Alexandra up short. She
couldn't start deluding herself. Nathan was her friend.
Period. It was foolish—indeed dangerous—to slot
him into a role that he hadn't signed up for. Their relationship was a figment of their imagination. That was
the way they both wanted it. The only way it could be.

"I think our Chloe is a natural. She'll be riding on
her own before long."

*Our Chloe.* Alexandra knew he didn't mean anything by the careless comment, but even still it warmed
her heart. It should have been a siren, providing a
warning of an upcoming danger. Yet somehow it
wasn't.

She wasn't looking for a daddy for Chloe. She
and her daughter were a complete family. They were
doing fine on their own. There might be a time in the
future when Alexandra met a man she would risk

her heart for. But that time wasn't now. And Nathan wasn't that man.

Just because there was no romantic future for them didn't mean she couldn't appreciate the kind of man he was. He was thoughtful and considerate. Gentle. With a physique that was second to none. He had the muscular body that came from hours spent doing hard, physical labor. Strength radiated from every pore of his body. He also possessed enough sex appeal to make her mouth water whenever he was around. Being near him made her entertain thoughts that had no business crossing her mind. He was her fake boyfriend. Given her desire to protect her heart, she shouldn't be thinking those thoughts about anyone.

Yet, she couldn't stop from fantasizing about how good it would feel to be held in his strong arms as she leaned her head against his solid chest and breathed in his masculine scent. And his thighs. They were so muscular. She felt her eyes straying to them, sneaking peeks when he wasn't looking. Nathan was everything a man should be. He was the man dreams were made of. Not the G-rated variety. She began to sweat as her imaginings grew even more erotic. A groan slipped out of her mouth and she bit her bottom lip.

Nathan glanced over and caught her staring. She felt her skin grow warm under his gaze and hoped like heck that her runaway thoughts weren't written on her face. She didn't want him to know she was lusting after him. One short step away from pouncing on him and having her wicked way.

It probably wasn't a new experience for him. Lots

of women had bid on the opportunity to have a date with him. But none of those women were staring at him hard enough to drill a hole in his magnificent body. She smiled.

"This is so much fun," she said, in an effort to cover up the fact that she had been staring at him.

"Even though we are moving at a snail's pace?"

"I suppose this is the best pace for Chloe."

"Not really. She's very secure. We can go a little bit faster. That is, if you're comfortable with the idea."

She nodded. "At first I was a little nervous about even putting her on a horse."

"That's completely understandable. She is your baby."

"Yes. But now, I'm not scared. I trust you not to let any harm come to my daughter."

He looked at her, as several expressions crossed his face in rapid succession. She saw shock and surprise quickly followed by pleasure and pride. When those emotions fled, they left an undecipherable expression behind.

Nathan gave her a tender smile. "Your little girl will always be safe with me."

A lump formed in her throat. She swallowed twice before she could speak. Even then, her voice was a raspy whisper. "I know. So we can go a little faster if you want."

He nodded. "Just a little."

He jiggled the reins and Excalibur went slightly faster. They weren't galloping or even trotting by any means, but they were going fast enough that Alexandra could actually tell that they were moving. Chloe cheered with happiness and then began gurgling as they slowly circled the corral.

After they'd made the circuit twice, Nathan turned and looked at Alexandra. "I think that is probably enough for now."

Alexandra sighed. She'd been enjoying this moment of freedom and relaxation. "Already?"

He nodded in Chloe's direction. "We don't want to overdo it."

He led Excalibur through the stable doors, and she followed on Snowflake. When they were inside, Alexandra slid from the back of the horse. She was about to take Chloe from Nathan when he dismounted, clearly unbothered by the little girl in his arms.

When he was on the ground, Chloe strained toward the horse. After it became clear that the ride was over, she began to fuss.

"Sorry," Alexandra said.

"Don't be," Nathan said, unfazed. He lifted Chloe over his head, releasing and then catching her several times. "I'm not pleased when I don't get my way. Believe me, if I could get away with crying, I would."

A startled laugh burst from Alexandra's lips. "That would be a sight to see."

Nathan grinned and lowered Chloe and held her against his chest. "I know you're upset little one, but we have a whole day planned. Okay?"

Chloe stopped fussing and frowned as if trying to understand what Nathan was saying. Then she threw her head back and laughed. After a moment, Nathan laughed with her.

"What's so funny?" Alexandra asked.

Nathan looked at Alexandra. "Sorry. That's a secret between us friends. Right, Chloe?"

Chloe nodded and babbled a reply.

"All right," Alexandra said. Foolishly, she felt left out.

Nathan brushed a kiss on Chloe's head, in much the way a father would, and then smiled at Alexandra. "You take the baby and I'll take care of the horses."

Alexandra held out her arms to Chloe. Generally her daughter would come to her eagerly, practically jumping into her arms. Instead, Chloe pursed her lips and then buried her head on Nathan's chest. Clearly her little girl was enchanted. Alexandra couldn't blame her. She would love to sink into Nathan's strong arms. Unlike Chloe, she couldn't be so bold. Alexandra doubted that Nathan would simply chuckle and rub her back.

"Come on, Chloe." Chloe didn't budge. Alexandra looked up at Nathan. "I don't know why she is acting this way."

"I guess she likes me."

"Of course she does. My daughter has good taste."

The slow, sexy smile that Nathan flashed her curled Alexandra's toes in her cowboy boots. They were only pretending to be in a relationship, but if she wasn't careful, she would fall in love with him. Then where would she be?

* * *

Nathan gave Chloe's back a final rub and then handed the little girl over to her mother. Chloe clung to him for a moment longer, before giving him a bright smile and releasing his shirt. Then she practically jumped into Alexandra's outstretched arms. That move nearly stopped his heart. The last thing he wanted was to drop the baby. Alexandra didn't bat an eye. Apparently Chloe's daredevil ways were nothing new to her.

He loved his nieces and nephew, but he'd never felt the same tenderness holding them that he felt for Chloe. When he'd learned that his date at the bachelor auction was a single mother, he'd been a little bit leery. Even though the date was supposed to be a onetime thing, he hadn't wanted to deal with someone who was looking for a daddy for her child. When he'd realized Alexandra wasn't looking for anything permanent, much less a father for her child, he'd been relieved.

Now though, it wasn't relief that he felt. After spending just a few minutes with Chloe, he felt a surprising protectiveness and attachment. Not that he was thinking of altering the plans for his life. He was not considering anything remotely like that. Being an uncle was enough for now.

And yet…

"I have her now," Alexandra said, pulling Nathan away from his musings.

Nathan nodded. As Alexandra's hands brushed

his, he felt a spark of electricity. He inhaled and the sensation traveled throughout his body, not sparing a single spot until his entire body was sending one message to his mind. He wanted more than a brush of hands from Alexandra. He wanted full body contact. Of course, that wouldn't be happening. Theirs was a relationship in name only.

He wasn't opposed to a purely physical relationship. He'd had a few in the past and they'd been mutually beneficial. But what he and Alexandra had was entirely different. They were becoming friends. That relationship would last much longer than one intense weekend. Therefore, he couldn't cross the line, no matter how tempting the notion was.

He reluctantly stepped away, removed the horses' saddles, then led them to their stalls. Nathan tried not to notice that Alexandra was following behind him, talking to Chloe as they kept up with him. She pointed out other horses and mentioned little details about them.

"This one is black," she said, coming up to Midnight. "Isn't he pretty?"

Chloe babbled in response.

"And this one has gray and white spots," Alexandra said.

Nathan told himself to focus on the task at hand, but it was hard to concentrate with Alexandra's sexy voice distracting him. It was low and appealing and sent his imagination into overdrive.

"This is just pretend," he said to himself softly. "So control yourself before you make a big mistake."

"Did you say something?" Alexandra asked, coming to stand in front of Excalibur's stall. As with the other horses, the door leading to the corral was open, so the horse could go in and out at will.

He gave the horse a final brush before exiting the stall and stepping into the aisle. "No. I was just talking to myself."

"I didn't mean to eavesdrop." She flashed him a sweet smile that sent the blood racing through his veins. That reaction was totally inappropriate for someone who was supposed to think of Alexandra as a friend. Especially since his five-year plan didn't include her.

"Not to worry. I wasn't saying anything that needs to be kept confidential."

She laughed and his heart lurched. Her laughter was carefree, and it reached a place inside him that previously hadn't existed. That part liked the idea of being with Alexandra on a more permanent basis. He quickly silenced that thought before it could take root in his head. Or heart.

"Come on. Let's go in the house. I think we could use a snack." And he could use a cold drink.

"Sounds good," Alexandra replied, oblivious to the way her nearness was tantalizing him.

As they walked to the house, Nathan caught himself sneaking looks at Alexandra. He loved the elegant way she moved. She didn't walk as much as she floated. The way her slender hips swayed was extremely sexy.

And enticing. She stepped close to him, and her sweet scent wafted around him.

He told himself to calm down and think of something else, but he couldn't stop his mind from fantasizing about spending intimate time with her. Why was it so hard to remember their relationship was purely a work of fiction?

When they stepped inside his house, Nathan grabbed Chloe's belongings and then led them into the kitchen. Alexandra took Chloe into the adjoining family room, set her on a plastic mat, and gave her a quick diaper change. Once that was done, she put Chloe on her play mat and gave her a couple of toys. Chloe ignored those and then crawled over to the mini piano Nathan kept for the nieces and nephew to play with when they visited. She plopped onto her diapered bottom and began pounding on the keys. After a moment, she began to sing.

"She's quite musical."

Alexandra laughed. "I don't know that she has much natural talent. Of course it might be too early to tell."

"Oh, I think she has pretty good pitch. And she's very comfortable in front of an audience."

"You can tell all of that?"

"I have some experience performing. Remember?"

"I'll never forget that story. Do you have any videos?"

"My mother does. She keeps them as blackmail material."

Alexandra shook her head. "She probably keeps them because she was proud of you and your brothers."

"That's what she claims, but I'm not fooled."

"Do you miss performing? Ever think of getting the band back together again?"

"God, no. It was fun when we were kids. But we're grown now."

"So you don't miss singing?"

"I still sing from time to time. Not in public, but around the house while I listen to the radio."

"If I turn on a song that you know, will you sing for me?" Her eyes widened as if she suddenly realized how intimate that question sounded.

"You mean, would I serenade you?" He didn't know why the idea suddenly held such appeal, but it did.

"I guess it probably sounds a little bit ridiculous."

"No. Actually, it doesn't." He told himself that he would sing for any of his friends if they asked, although it wasn't true. He never sang for anyone. "You pick a song and I'll gladly sing it for you."

She smiled. "Now I feel like the pressure is really on me."

"Why would the pressure be on you?"

"Because. Now I have to come up with the perfect song. Are you partial to any type of music? Would you prefer a ballad? Or would you prefer an up-tempo song?"

"It really doesn't matter. Just name a song that you like and I'll sing it. If I don't know it, I'll learn it."

Her face lit up with pleasure. She was positively radiant. "Are you serious? You're willing to do all of that? For me?"

"Yes." Nathan would sing for her. He'd do anything to make her happy.

And that truth was more than a little unsettling.

## Chapter Thirteen

Alexandra tried to slow her racing heart. Nathan wasn't making a big deal about singing to her, so why was she? For all she knew, he sang for women all the time. That thought bothered her more than it should have. After all, she and Nathan were only pretending, so it shouldn't matter to her if he sang to every woman in Colorado. They weren't in love.

Chloe stopped "playing" and "singing" and then got on all fours and crawled over to Alexandra. When Chloe reached her, Alexandra took her hands and then helped her to stand. "That's a big girl. Look who's standing up."

Chloe chortled and then began bouncing up and down, laughing happily as she did so.

"Hey," Nathan said. Chloe tried to drop on all fours, but Alexandra kept holding her hands. "Let's walk."

"Can she walk on her own?"

"Yes. But she prefers to crawl."

"I suppose she wants to stick with the familiar."

"Crawling is faster. My little girl is impatient to get where she wants. She's all about speed."

He laughed and the sound raised goose bumps on her arms. She didn't understand why she was having such a hard time ignoring her attraction to him. Generally, once she made up her mind, it was done. She didn't waste time waffling. There was no second-guessing. She'd already decided that there was no room in her life for a man. That should be the end of it. So why wasn't it?

Now she found herself fighting feelings that she hadn't expected to have. And they were growing stronger with every moment that she spent with him.

The rational part of her wondered if she should end the farce before it got out of hand. Falling for him wasn't part of the plan. So she was going to knock it off. He was just a friend. And that was how she was going to think of him from now on.

"Do you need help in the kitchen?"

"No. I actually enjoy cooking. I find it quite relaxing. I try to cook as often as I can."

"What's your favorite thing to make?"

"I don't really have a favorite. It's more that I go through phases."

"What do you mean?"

"There was a time that I was all about French foods. I'm talking everything from coq au vin to Crepe Suzette. Then I was all about Greek food. Then seafood."

"Really? That's interesting. What are we having for lunch?"

"Given the fact that we have a little one with us, I thought we would have grilled cheese. It's a favorite of the little people in our family." His brow wrinkled. "She can eat grilled cheese, can't she?"

"Yes. She's almost one so she can eat a lot of finger foods, as long as they're cut into very small pieces."

"I have American cheese, but I also have mozzarella."

"Oh. I think she would like that."

"I'm going to make chicken and vegetable stir-fry for us."

"Oh. I like the sound of that."

"Then sit down and keep me company. I did all of the prep work earlier, so this will be a piece of cake."

Alexandra sat in one of the chairs at the island and held Chloe in her lap. She handed Chloe a stuffed toy and then watched as her daughter played with it. The moment felt so quiet. So normal. They could have been a family. Of course they weren't, and she reminded herself not to get caught up in a fantasy world.

Nathan and Alexandra talked as he prepared lunch. When it was done, he put the food on the table. He grabbed a high chair from the pantry and set it beside Alexandra's chair. She gave him a puzzled look.

He shrugged. "Remember, I have little ones over for dinner from time to time. It was easier and much neater to buy a high chair and booster seats than to let them eat at the coffee table in the family room, even though they seem to prefer that."

"Of course. That must seem like an adventure to them. They probably don't get to eat like that at home."

"They just like to roam as they eat. Strapping them in saves my walls and keeps the mess in one place."

"You definitely have thought of everything. I didn't have you pegged as a man who would flip out over a little dirt. After all, you are a rancher, and that can be pretty dirty from what I've seen."

"You're right. Which is why the boots stay at the door. No need to drag that mess all through the house. And if my clothes get too dirty, I drop them there too."

Alexandra immediately pictured a nearly nude Nathan standing before her, and her mouth began to water even as she broke out into a cold sweat. She grabbed her glass and took a long drink of iced tea.

"The stir-fry isn't too spicy, is it?"

She shook her head. "No. It's perfect. I like my food with a little kick to it."

"So do I." Nathan gave her a look before picking up his own fork.

Alexandra broke eye contact and glanced over at Chloe, who was happily chewing on her sandwich. Nathan had cut it into small slices, so it was just the right size for her little hands. Alexandra set a sippy cup of apple juice on the tray so Chloe could grab that whenever she wanted. She appeared content, so Alexandra turned her attention back to her food. But even as she ate, satisfying one hunger, she knew that the other hunger—the one that was suddenly a longing for physical contact with Nathan—would have to go unfulfilled.

Nathan seemed completely unaware of the lust that he was inspiring, eating his meal with gusto. The stir-fry was delicious. The chicken was tender and the vegetables were crunchy. Even so, Alexandra's ego took a hit as she realized the desire was one-sided. Oh, she knew that Nathan was attracted to her. The kisses they'd shared were proof of that. But she was realistic enough to know his passion might be the result of a sexual dry spell. He'd told her that he hadn't been in a relationship for a while. He might have kissed any woman that way.

The thing was, the desire she was experiencing wasn't a generic longing for physical touch. It was a specific desire for a particular man. She was lusting over Nathan. No other man would have the same effect on her.

"So, have you made up your mind about staying in Aspen Creek?"

Alexandra frowned. "I haven't given it much thought."

"Ahh," he said as if she'd said something profound.

"What does that mean?"

"It's simple, really. The fact that you haven't given it any more thought appears to me that you have reached a decision."

"Really?" She held her fork suspended in midair, although she really wanted to put that water chestnut into her mouth. "And what decision would that be?"

"You're staying," he said confidently.

"How did you reach that conclusion?"

"The debate is over. That's why you aren't thinking about it. You feel comfortable in Aspen Creek and now it's home to you and Chloe. If it wasn't, you would still be trying to figure out your next move."

"You think?"

"Yes. You stopped looking for home because you've found it."

Had she? "Maybe. But my family is in Chicago. If Chloe and I move here, she won't see my parents, brother, and sister nearly as often as she would if we went back. Their relationships will suffer. And Chloe is the only grandchild."

He nodded. "That is a consideration. As someone who lives on the same piece of land as my parents and brothers, I understand how important family is. I can't imagine not seeing them as often as I do. Physical nearness is important."

"True. But it's not as if we're estranged. We can always visit each other. And I do feel at home here. As if I belong."

"I'm not surprised. Aspen Creek is just that kind of place. There is a sense of community. You and Chloe have made friends. You have a job you love, you have your aunt and a home. Why keep looking when you've found everything you want right here?"

"That's a good point."

"That's the only kind I make."

She laughed and resumed eating. "Oh, you are so full of yourself."

"That comes from being the oldest child. I always knew more than my little brothers."

"I bet you were a bossy big brother."

He gave a grin that made her heart lurch. "To hear them tell it, I still am."

"Really?"

"It comes from a place of love. Wanting to protect them. I can't stand by and watch them make mistakes without saying something."

"So you're trying to run their lives."

"Not at all. I give my opinion and then let them do what they are going to do. If it blows up in their faces, they can't say that I didn't warn them."

"And if it doesn't blow up in their faces? If it works out just the way they wanted it to? The way they expected it to?"

He shrugged his massive shoulders. "Then no harm no foul."

"Oh. Spoken just like a big brother. You guys are all so annoying."

"We come that way from the factory."

"You're blaming factory settings?"

"Only because it happens to be true. Big brothers know from the minute that our younger siblings are born that we have a responsibility to care for them. All good big brothers do just that."

She rolled her eyes. "You have got to be kidding me."

"Answer this. If it's not too personal."

She nodded. "Go ahead."

"How did your brother feel about Chloe's father?"

"Oh. That is a question."

"And if it is too nosy, please just ignore it. And forgive me."

She smiled. He sounded serious. And worried. "It's not too nosy. And I don't mind answering. The truth is he didn't like Owen. He never came out and said the words. And he was always cordial. But he never treated Owen in the joking manner that he treated my sister's boyfriend. Or even some of my previous boyfriends. I guess I should have known there was a reason. But he never said. And I never asked."

He nodded. "It's hard to know what to do in those circumstances. You want to keep your siblings safe, but you know there's a line you can't cross and still have a good relationship with them. And no matter how it seems, we want to have good relationships with our younger siblings."

"I know. But when you're in the middle of it, you don't want to hear it."

"Which is why it's so hard to be a big brother."

"I'll give you that point."

He smiled. They had finished eating, so Nathan stood and picked up their plates. Chloe had eaten all of her grilled cheese sandwich and apple slices. She picked up her cup with both handles and then leaned back, noisily guzzling the last of her juice. When she finished, she dropped the cup onto the tray and let out a loud burp.

"Good one," Nathan said with a laugh.

"I've been trying to teach her table manners, but so far she hasn't caught on." Alexandra picked up

Chloe. "If you'll excuse us for a moment. I need to wash up this little one."

"Take your time. I need to clean up the kitchen."

Alexandra held Chloe tight as she walked down the hall, being careful to keep her daughter from touching anything with her greasy hands. The last thing she wanted to do was create a dirty mess on his pristine walls. There were no pictures on the wall, which, given the beautiful artwork in the rest of the house, was a bit disappointing. Even so, the house had the same impact on her today as it had the first time she'd seen it. It was stylish without being showy. Comfortable. The overflowing toy box in the family room was evidence that he wanted everyone to feel welcome here. Even the ones with sticky hands.

She wiped Chloe's face and hands and then they went back to the kitchen. Chloe looked around, then began straining against Alexandra's chest, struggling to get down. Nathan was in the family room, digging through the toy box. There was a pile of toys at his feet, but he was pulling out even more. A couple of them were playing music and Chloe pressed more forcefully against Alexandra's chest.

Nathan glanced up. When he saw them, he smiled. His charming, boyish grin was almost sheepish. "I thought she might want to play for a while."

"You obviously know the way to Chloe's heart. She loves playing with musical toys." Alexandra stepped into the family room and then set her daughter onto the floor. Chloe immediately crawled across the room until she reached a musical ball. The minute she touched it, the ball rolled away from her. Not one to back away from a challenge, Chloe crawled after it. When she reached it, she slapped her hand on it, causing it to roll away. She let out a loud cry of frustration and began chasing it again.

"Looks like somebody needs help," Nathan said. He sat down on the floor, blocking the ball with his leg. Chloe crawled over and hit it again, but this time the ball couldn't escape. She laughed and then hit the ball over and over. With each touch, the song changed. Chloe plopped onto her diapered bottom and hit the ball over again.

Alexandra crossed the room and sat on the floor across from Nathan. Whenever the ball rolled away from Chloe, one of them would send the ball back into her direction, keeping her happy. After a few minutes, Chloe grew bored with the ball. Without missing a beat, Nathan picked up a stuffed giraffe and handed it to Chloe. She took the toy and smiled at Nathan. Then she crawled over to Alexandra and climbed on her lap, leaning her head against Alexandra's breasts.

"It looks like someone is getting sleepy," Nathan said.

It was naptime, so Alexandra wasn't surprised. Truthfully, she was glad to have a child who stuck to her schedule more often than not. Now though, Alexandra wasn't ready for the date to end and she wished that Chloe would stay awake a little while longer.

"Do you want to let her sleep on the couch for a

bit? That way you can keep an eye on her and we can hang out longer. I don't have a crib since the grandparents are generally the ones who keep the kids overnight. Or would you rather I take you home so she can sleep in her own bed?"

Nathan watched as Alexandra contemplated his question. A few long seconds had passed and she still hadn't responded. He was trying not to show how much her answer meant to him. He might be able to hide his feelings from Alexandra, but he couldn't hide them from himself. He wanted her to stay. That was troubling. The emotions she awoke within him were unexpected. Though he had no plans of becoming involved romantically with a woman now, his feelings weren't entirely unwanted. Alexandra was making him go against his plan.

Now he had trouble thinking clearly where she was concerned. It wasn't that he'd stopped believing in the perfect order of things. He still believed there was a time and place for everything. It was just that he was beginning to wonder if he might need to make adjustments to the order. Maybe there were different times and places for the big events in his life than he had once believed.

Nathan blinked. That thought was not something he'd wanted to entertain for long, yet he couldn't totally rid himself of it. Was he really thinking about reorganizing his entire life simply because he was attracted to Alexandra? That didn't make a lick of sense.

He barely knew her. They'd only gone on two dates—three if you counted today. Besides, he'd been attracted to a lot of women in his life. Sometimes he'd acted on that attraction. Other times he hadn't. But never once had he even considered reordering his life.

"Well, to be honest," Alexandra said, pulling Nathan out of his disturbing thoughts. "Chloe would be doing a lot of her sleeping in her car seat. If you don't mind letting her lie on your couch, I am happy hanging out with you for a while longer."

He breathed an internal sigh of relief. He knew he was getting in over his head, but he didn't know how to dial it back. Nor was he sure he wanted to. Truth be told, he enjoyed having Alexandra around. He wanted to look at her beautiful face for a while longer. He wanted to listen to her sweet voice and inhale her intoxicating scent. He could catalog the varied things he was finding pleasure in, but honestly, he wanted to enjoy *all* of her.

"In that case, let me grab a sheet and blanket so our little angel can sleep more comfortably."

"Thanks."

Nathan jogged upstairs to the linen closet. He grabbed a sheet and a blanket, then returned to the family room. Alexandra was standing beside the window, swaying back and forth as she rocked Chloe the rest of the way to sleep. Her back was to him and he took a moment to admire her shapely figure. She was so sexy in her jeans and blouse. Alexandra must have sensed his presence because she turned around. When their eyes met, she gave him a soft smile. His heart squeezed, and for a moment, he was mesmerized by her and could only stare. He was struck not just by her beauty, but by her aura. There was a sweetness and calmness to her that touched him.

Chloe stirred and Alexandra brushed a kiss across her head. "She's just about fallen asleep."

That comment was a call to action, and Nathan strode into the family room. He covered one of the cushions with a sheet, then stepped aside so that Alexandra could lay Chloe down. She hovered a minute, watching as the baby stirred, moving around until she was comfortable. Chloe placed a thumb into her mouth and then was still. Smiling, Nathan covered her with a thin blanket. A tenderness swept through him, and he brushed a hand across her hair before stepping back.

"So..." he said, totally at a loss at what to say.

"So," Alexandra echoed.

Nathan shook his head in an attempt to get back on track. Alexandra hadn't agreed to stay here so he could gawk at her. Suddenly having Alexandra and Chloe around felt too natural. Too real. "Do you want something else to drink? Or maybe something to eat?"

"No, I'm fine."

Of course she wasn't hungry. They'd just eaten. He grabbed a couple of cushions from the large sectional and placed them on the floor in front of a sleeping Chloe. When Alexandra gave him a puzzled look he shrugged. "In case she rolls around, we'll be here to stop her fall."

"Good idea."

Sitting, he stretched his legs in front of him. Alexandra did the same. She was sitting close to him and the warmth from her body reached out, touching him and raising his temperature. Suddenly his mind was filled with images of the kisses they'd shared and a desire to kiss her again. His longing was a drumbeat inside him, growing stronger by the minute. His attraction to her and his desire for her was becoming an all-consuming force.

That was a problem.

How could he be around Alexandra and pretend to be in a relationship with her if the more time he spent with her, the more he wanted the relationship to become real? Just thinking about this puzzle gave him a headache.

"Why are you shaking your head?" Alexandra asked. There was a touch of humor in her voice.

He shook his head again and then laughed. He must look quite foolish to her. "You must think there is something wrong with me. First you see me talking to myself, and now I'm shaking my head."

She chuckled. "I was just wondering if it took you that long to answer yourself."

He grimaced. "I didn't know that you were so funny."

She dipped her head in a bow and then gestured her hand with a flourish. "I'm here all week."

And just like that, the lust that he had been trying to extinguish reignited. Their conversation faded away, and she seemed just as incapable of picking up the threads as he was. The truth was, he didn't want to talk. There was only one thing on his mind.

Their eyes met and he recognized the longing in hers. There was no use denying the serious attraction between them. And he was tired of fighting it. They were already sitting close enough to touch, but she leaned even closer to him. Her intent was clear, but still, he hesitated. Didn't move. He needed her to make the first move. She reached out and touched his face with trembling fingers. That soft contact was all it took to break through his self-control. He moved closer and brushed his lips across hers.

From the second their lips met, he knew the kiss was going to be hot. She opened her mouth to him and he swept inside. She tasted just as sweet as he remembered. But mingled with that sweetness was a fiery desire that matched his.

He slid an arm beneath her knees and his other behind her back, lifting her onto his lap. She wrapped her arms around his neck and they deepened the kiss. Time paused and then stood still. On and on the kiss went, until she broke away. He was panting too hard to do more than stare at her, his eyes asking the question that he was unable to voice. Why had she pulled back?

She pressed her palms against her chest, then answered his unspoken question. "I think that we're getting carried away here. This is supposed to be a pretend relationship. Making out like a couple of horny teenagers—as pleasurable as it is—is out of bounds."

Try as he might, he couldn't find an argument to dispute her. Perhaps because she was right. He nodded. She slid off his lap, and although his body was screaming for him not to let her go, he resisted the urge to pull her back into his arms.

"This is so much harder than I expected. You are so irresistible."

She giggled and looked directly at him. Longing still lingered in her eyes. "I know. Right? What is that?"

"I don't know. We're just incredibly attracted to each other." He knew that he could reignite the fire between them again with one kiss. But he respected her too much to try.

"Annoying, isn't it?"

He nodded. That was one thing that he appreciated about Alexandra. One of many things. She understood the situation and didn't try to make it something that it wasn't. They were attracted to each other. Not in love.

"I suppose we should come up with a way to keep this under control," he said.

"That sounds like a good idea. Do you have a plan? Because I sure don't." Her expression was so open and honest. So irresistible.

"No. But if we are going to convince my family that we are a couple, I suppose our mutual attraction isn't a bad thing. We need to be comfortable with each other." It was a stretch, but he had to come up with a reason why it was a good thing he couldn't keep his hands off her. A reason that didn't involve his heart.

"And the best way to be comfortable is to practice," she said, taking his idea and running with it. Her eyes sparkled with mischief.

"And practice makes perfect. I am nothing if not a perfectionist."

"I don't like to do things halfway either."

He wondered if that meant she would go all the way, as the kids used to say in high school. He knew better than to ask because he didn't want to press his luck. Truthfully, he didn't know what answer was worse—*yes* or *no*. "So I guess that explains everything."

"Yep." She ran a hand over her hair, straightening it the best she could without a comb. His hands ached to experience the pleasure of running through her hair again, so he curled them into fists. He had been creeping up to the line, and he knew that the wise thing to do was back away before he crossed it.

They continued to speak quietly for a while, enjoying each other's company.

Chloe stirred and he and Alexandra turned as one to look at her. As if feeling their gazes, the baby opened her eyes and gave them a sleepy stare before closing her eyes again.

"It won't be long before she wakes up," Alexandra said. "She'll be groggy for a few minutes, but then she'll be ready to play again."

"Will she be hungry?"

"Yes. I have a snack packed for her. And, of course, a diaper change." She paused briefly. "Unless you're ready for us to go home. We don't want to overstay our welcome."

"You aren't. That's why I invited you to stay while Chloe slept. It would be nice to spend a few more hours together if you don't have other plans."

"I don't have anything planned. Just dinner and playing with Chloe for a while. But you have toys here so that would be all that we need."

Chloe made a sound and they looked at her again. Her eyes were wide-open and she was smiling. She sat up and reached out to Alexandra.

Alexandra took her daughter into her embrace and kissed her chubby cheeks. "Look who's awake. I bet you want a new diaper."

Nathan reached into her diaper bag and pulled out a diaper as well as the vinyl mat. "I bet you could use this."

She took them from him. "Thanks."

He grabbed the sheet and blanket and then stood. "I'll give you some privacy."

"Thanks."

"Oh, and if you're free, would you like to have dinner at my parents' next Sunday? My brothers and their families will be there. I know you met them briefly at Miles and Jillian's wedding, but this will be a good opportunity for you to get to know everyone better."

She paused and then smiled. "I guess the plan is no good if we don't put it into practice."

"Is that a yes?"

She hesitated, and he held his breath, waiting until she answered. "Yes. We would love to have dinner with you and your family."

## Chapter Fourteen

The following Sunday, Alexandra stood on Nathan's parents' front porch and looked around the sprawling ranch. There were acres of land with trees interspersed over the otherwise flat land. Naturally the mountains were visible in the distance. The view was spectacular, but she preferred the scenery around Nathan's house.

This house was more in keeping with what she thought a ranch house would look like. It was a large, sprawling, redbrick building with a wide front porch. Several chairs were grouped around a wicker and glass table on one side of the wide staircase. A swing and several rocking chairs were on the other. She could imagine sitting on the swing and looking out over the large lawn, sipping lemonade in the summer and hot chocolate in the fall.

She forced the cozy image away. She wasn't going

to become a part of this family, so those peaceful evenings weren't going to be a part of her future. Once she and Nathan convinced his mother that they were involved, he wouldn't need her any longer. They could stage a breakup, then go back to their normal lives. Lives that didn't include each other.

When she'd agreed to pretend to be his girlfriend, she hadn't anticipated everything that would be involved. She'd imagined that they would have a few dates in popular spots where they would be seen. Word would get back to his mother that Nathan had a girlfriend, and that would be the end of it. Instead, she was about to sit down to a family dinner.

After their date last Saturday, Nathan had come to visit her twice during the week. She'd cooked dinner once, and he'd picked up carryout from a restaurant in town the other time. Nathan had insisted that the dates were important so that they could honestly say they were spending time together. Besides, he wanted to work on their cover story. Alexandra had to admit that she'd enjoyed her pretend dates a whole lot more than she had some real dates. They might be pretending, but Nathan was behaving like a real boyfriend. If she was interested in dating, he was exactly the type of man that she would want to be involved with.

He had also called her a few times during the week just to talk. They'd talked long into the night about Chloe's upcoming birthday party—Nathan had volunteered the ranch, but Alexandra decided to have the party at her aunt's house. They also discussed the big deal he was close to finalizing. Once again, he'd claimed that the phone calls were necessary in order to make their story realistic. Not that they needed to be all that creative. It was common knowledge that she and Nathan had met at the bachelor auction, so they didn't have to come up with a meet-cute.

Alexandra took a deep breath and then glanced up at Nathan. Suddenly she suffered a bout of nerves. She had never been much of an actress. The only time she'd been onstage had been third grade when she'd played an elf in the Christmas program. She'd forgotten her lines and had all but broken into tears. She knew that this wasn't entirely the same thing— she wasn't an eight-year-old explaining how toys were made—but she would be putting on an act.

Luckily, she wasn't alone. She had Nathan by her side. He could feed her lines to her if she got stuck. More than that, he wouldn't stand by silently and let his family grill her. Not that she expected a grilling. But she knew the drill. She'd met enough families of boyfriends to know that there would be some gentle questioning. If they got along well enough, there would be a bit of good-natured teasing.

She also had her secret weapon—Chloe. Her little girl was quite the charmer. Very few people could resist her. When she smiled, even the coldest heart melted. If Chloe became fussy, Alexandra would have the perfect excuse to take a break from the group.

"Ready?" Nathan asked.

"Yes." She smiled up at him. He looked so gorgeous in his blue shirt, black jeans, and his ever-present cowboy hat. Tingles raced down her spine. One thing was certain. She wouldn't have to fake her attraction. "I'm just trying to get a handle on my nerves."

"Why are you nervous?" He seemed genuinely confused.

"Because I want to make a good impression. I want your family to like me. Or at least not sit there wondering what in the world you see in me."

He brushed a gentle kiss on her cheek. She knew that he intended the kiss to be comforting. And it was. But it also stirred up longing inside her. A small part of her that refused to be silenced wished that this pretend relationship was actually a real one. The more time she spent with Nathan, the more she was coming to see that he was the real deal. Authentic. The kind of man that a woman could look for forever and not find. Yet here she was with him. And not with him.

Not that it mattered. She might be coming to care about him, but that didn't mean that he was also doing an about-face. The rational part of her believed that was a good thing. She already had enough balls in the air. She couldn't juggle another one.

"My family liked you when they met you at the reception. Once they know you better, they will love you. After all, what is there not to love?"

She felt herself blushing. "You had better dial back the charm."

He laughed and leaned in closer. "Why would I do something like that?"

She looked away. There was no way that she was going to tell him that she was starting to fall for him. Especially not when they were about to step into his parents' home. Neither of them needed that kind of pressure. The situation was fraught enough already.

Before she could think of a suitable reply, the front door swung open. Alexandra turned and looked into Nathan's brother's face. She recalled meeting Isaac at the reception. Even if she hadn't met him before, she would know they were brothers. The resemblance was strong.

"Hey. I saw your car out the window a few minutes ago. We're about to start taking bets on whether you plan to come inside or make a break for it."

"How was it looking?" Nathan asked.

"Not good. That's why I opened the door." He turned to Alexandra. "I don't know if you remember me from the reception. Come on in, I'm Isaac—"

"Of course. Nathan's brother. I remember you. And thank you," Alexandra said, stepping inside the house, Nathan right behind her. Chloe leaned back as she tried to see the two-story ceiling. Alexandra put her hand on Chloe's back to make sure that her little girl didn't tumble from her arms.

They stepped inside the living room where the family was gathered. For a moment, Alexandra was a bit nervous. She'd been honest when she'd said that she wanted Nathan's family to think well of her for his sake. But that had only been part of the truth. She also wanted them to like her for herself.

"Welcome," Nathan's mother said with a smile. "We didn't get to talk much at the reception. Hopefully we can remedy that."

The smile on the other woman's face was warm and

welcoming, and Alexandra immediately felt at ease. "I look forward to that, Mrs. Montgomery."

"Please, call me Michelle."

"I will." Alexandra looked around. "I'm looking forward to getting to know all of you better. Nathan has told me a lot of good things about his family."

Isaac snorted and Alexandra wondered if she had gone too far. But when she saw the laughter in his eyes, she remembered that he was the jokester of the family.

Nathan quickly reintroduced the rest of his family. Alexandra smiled a greeting to each of them before she set Chloe on the sofa and retied her shoelace before picking her up again. The littles, as Nathan referred to his nieces and nephew, immediately rushed over to them.

"Baby," said a little girl who didn't look much older than Chloe.

"Yes, she is," Savannah said. She winked at Alexandra and then whispered, "Isn't it funny how little kids are so willing to call another kid a baby. But then, I guess to Mia she is."

"How old is your little girl?" Alexandra asked.

"A year and a half."

"She's a cutie."

"Thank you. She's also a handful."

"I like your baby," the other little girl said. Alexandra recognized her as the flower girl, Lilliana.

"Thank you."

"Bye," Lilliana said, abruptly. Then she and Benji turned and ran away. Lilliana looked back. "Come on, Mia."

Mia tugged on Savannah's arm, held her face up, and pursed her lips. "Kiss, Mommy."

Savannah kissed the toddler and then watched as her little girl chased after the other kids.

Jillian walked over to them. "It's good to see you again. We didn't get to talk much at the reception."

"I understand how that goes. The bride is always the star of the show and in demand. Your wedding was beautiful, by the way."

"Thank you. I had a great time. But the reason we didn't get to talk had more to do with Nathan than anything else. He monopolized your time. It was as if he didn't want to share you with anyone else."

Alexandra felt her cheeks growing warm as she reflected back on the reception. She and Nathan had spent nearly every moment by each other's side. Time had seemed to fly with each pleasurable hour. She couldn't believe it when the band leader had announced the last dance. "Nathan is kind that way. He knew that I didn't know any other people and didn't want me to feel uncomfortable."

It also cut down on the risk that one of them would make a mistake that would blow the whole charade before they even started.

Savannah and Jillian exchanged glances and Alexandra realized that she hadn't fooled either one of them. But then, perhaps that was for the best. She and Nathan were supposed to be convincing his family that they were in a serious relationship.

"Is that what you really think?" Jillian asked.

Alexandra laughed. She had a feeling that she was

going to like Savannah and Jillian quite a bit. "Not really. But given the way our relationship started, I wasn't going to get my hopes up."

"I understand completely," Savannah said. "It's hard to put your heart out there. There is always the fear that it will get broken."

Jillian nodded in agreement, and Alexandra wondered what kind of heartaches they had suffered. Given the fact that neither of them was a teenager, it was likely that they had suffered heartbreak of one type or another. That was just the way life went. Alexandra had endured her own pain from a broken romance. But unlike Jillian and Savannah, she hadn't found that one person who made taking the risk worth it. Given the fact that she was no longer interested in love, she wouldn't find that someone for quite a while. Being with Nathan gave her all the benefits of having a man in her life without taking the risk associated with a failed relationship.

"But when you find the right one, you discover that it was worth the risk," Jillian said. She was practically glowing and a newlywed, so clearly she'd found that man in Miles.

Chloe squirmed to get down, so Alexandra set her on the floor near her feet where she could keep an eye on her. But Chloe had other ideas and immediately crawled over to Nathan. When she reached Nathan, he immediately picked her up. She chortled happily and placed her head on his chest.

"Someone is going to be spoiled," Savannah said. "I can see it now."

"Chloe really adores Nathan. He's so good with her."

"Nathan was all business before, so it's good to see him have more in his life than the ranch."

"The ranch is important to him," Alexandra said, feeling oddly protective of him. "It takes a lot of work to keep it going. And Nathan is not the type to let others pull his weight."

"Hey, nobody is criticizing his choices," Jillian said, laughing. "I've known Nathan all of my life. He's been a good friend to me. Even when Miles and I weren't on speaking terms, Nathan and I kept in touch. I'm just glad that he's found someone that makes him happy. Someone who can help him see that he can find happiness outside of the ranch he loves so much."

"Oh." Alexandra felt sheepish. "I guess I jumped to conclusions. I'm sorry."

"Don't be," Savannah said. "We're both very protective of our Montgomery men."

"We'd wonder what was up if you didn't come to his defense," Jillian added.

Before Alexandra could reply, Nathan's parents announced that dinner was on the table.

"We helped," Lilliana said.

"We did a good job," Benji said, proudly.

Mia nodded and then clapped her hands.

"I can only imagine how much help they were," Jillian said.

"Should I have offered to help?" Alexandra said. She wanted to make a good impression after all, and sitting on her hands while others worked was definitely not the way to do it.

Savannah shook her head. "We helped a lot when we arrived so there was very little left to do. The kids' idea of helping is eating half an oatmeal cookie that we aren't supposed to know about."

"Really? Before dinner?"

"Grandparents' privilege," Jillian said. "Besides it's only about three bites. And it comes with the condition that they eat their vegetables, so it all comes out in the wash."

Alexandra thought of her own parents and recalled how they enjoyed spoiling Chloe. Of course, her daughter had been so young at the time and didn't have any memories of them, or of how special they had made her feel. That was one of the hardest parts of leaving home and moving to Aspen Creek. Breaking the bonds of a relationship that is so important to everyone.

Not that her family was out of their lives. She spoke with her parents several times a week and at least once a week with her brother and sister. And unless something unexpected happened, Alexandra's parents planned to come to town for Chloe's birthday party in two weeks. Even if they managed to come to town for a visit, Chloe wouldn't enjoy the regular spoiling that she would have gotten if she lived closer to her family.

Getting everyone around the table was a bit hectic, and there was good-natured teasing as Isaac sat beside Alexandra, pulling Savannah into the empty seat on his other side. Then Miles sat on Alexandra's other side, keeping Nathan from sitting beside her.

"Funny guys," Nathan said.

"We thought so," Miles said, getting to his feet.

"No matter how old we get, little brothers are a nuisance," Nathan said.

Everyone laughed at Nathan's put-out look, and Alexandra found herself joining in. After the blessing was said, everyone began serving themselves. Nathan explained that his mother usually had the children eat at the same table as the adults, but Benji and Lilliana had spent a lot of time with the other grandparents while Miles and Jillian had been on their honeymoon. Those grandparents let them use their own table for lunch and snacks. Somehow they had convinced Michelle to let them eat at their own table today. Chloe, however, still used a high chair and she was enjoying her bits of macaroni, chicken, and greens with the adults.

"Is the baby going to eat with us?" Lilliana asked.

"No. She needs a special chair," Alexandra said.

Lilliana shot Chloe a look that could only be described as pity before turning in her chair to eat the food Jillian had set in front of her.

"They like having their own table," Jillian said, taking her chair at the table.

"I remember sitting at the kid's table," Alexandra said. "But I recall wanting to eat at the big table for the longest time."

"Kids these days are made different," Isaac said. "They like having their own place."

"So Lilliana can talk Benji into doing something

that will land them both in trouble," Jillian said with a grin.

"Like mother, like daughter," Nathan said, before turning to Alexandra to explain. "Miles and Jillian were friends as kids. She was always getting him into trouble. Lilliana is like the second coming of Jillian, and Benji is as laid-back as Miles was."

The conversation continued and Alexandra was instantly included. In only a few minutes time, she felt comfortable enough to join in the kidding and laughing. She glanced at Nathan and caught him staring at her, an intense expression on his face. The look made her heart pound and the blood in her veins began to pulse rapidly.

The surroundings faded away and Alexandra was only aware of Nathan. The deep, rich brown of his eyes, framed by dark, curly lashes. The way one eyebrow was raised just a smidge. The deep dimples in his cheeks. The warmth from his body reaching out to her. They were sitting so close that their shoulders brushed as they ate. It wasn't annoying. Quite the opposite. She liked it. His touch increased her attraction to him.

Chloe banged her cup on the table, and Alexandra immediately became aware of her surroundings. She looked away from Nathan and caught a glimpse of Isaac's expression. He was smirking as if he'd caught her and Nathan doing something wrong. Alexandra looked from him to her daughter. "What do you need, sweetie?"

Chloe babbled and then held out her cup.

"Looks like she wants more milk," Nathan said, coming to his feet. "I'll get her a refill."

"Thanks," Alexandra said.

"Who would have thought that Nathan would be so good with a baby?" Jillian asked.

"Certainly not me," Miles said. "Especially after the way he looked the first time we left Lilliana and Benji with him."

Everyone laughed.

"How did he look?" Alexandra asked.

"Like he had run ten miles," Jillian said.

"Nah. He looked like he'd been run over by a truck," Miles added.

There was more laughter as Nathan returned to the room. Chloe reached out for the cup, which he instantly placed into her hands. Then he placed a kiss on her head before sitting back down.

"What's so funny?" he asked.

"They were telling me about the first time that you babysat Lilliana and Benji."

He chuckled and shook his head. "Don't let those kids fool you. They may seem sweet and innocent, sitting there and eating like normal people, but let me tell you. They never stopped moving. Climbing all over the furniture. Trying to find trouble to get into. I have never been so tired. Those were the longest two days of my life."

Laughing, Jillian corrected him. "It was maybe an hour or so."

"That's not better," Nathan said. "It just goes to show how exhausting they were."

"How are you going to handle it when Chloe starts running and climbing?" Miles asked.

Alexandra sucked in a breath as she waited for Nathan to respond. She knew this was only a fake relationship, but she couldn't stop her very real reaction.

"Chloe is a perfect angel, so I don't have to worry about her getting into any kind of mischief."

"Keep dreaming," Jillian said. Then she turned to Alexandra. "No offense."

"None taken." Alexandra replied.

"I'll tolerate no Chloe slander at this table," Nathan said.

Everyone laughed, and the conversation switched to other topics. Though Alexandra knew that Nathan was only pretending, her heart warmed at the affection he showed her daughter.

"Did you have a good time?" Nathan asked Alexandra as they stepped inside her house a few hours later. Chloe had fallen asleep on the way home and Nathan was holding her in his arms as Alexandra closed the door behind them.

"I did. Your family is great."

"They felt the same about you."

She smiled and his heart skipped a beat. Though he'd been with Alexandra all day, he still hadn't become immune to her presence. Everything about her was enticing. From the way she nibbled her bottom lip when she was thinking to the way she tossed her hair over her shoulder when she laughed. There were so many things that he liked about her. So many more things that he wanted to learn. But that would take commitment, something neither of them wanted.

"I guess your plan worked. You don't have to worry about your mother setting you up on blind dates."

He didn't know why that comment bothered him. True, that was what this whole charade was supposed to be about. But several times during the day, he'd forgotten they were only pretending to care about each other. It had begun to feel very real. He'd been so proud of the way she'd fit in with everyone. His mother had been won over when Alexandra had insisted on helping to clear the table. His father had been impressed by her knowledge of sports. Jillian and Savannah had each told him how much they liked Alexandra. Isaac and Miles had also told him that he'd made a good choice. The littles had adored her and Chloe. Once Chloe could keep up with the others, he could picture the threesome turning into a foursome.

That is, if the relationship was real. Which it wasn't.

Alexandra's words were appropriate given the situation, so he nodded. "Even so, I don't think we should stop seeing each other. That would make them suspicious."

"I agree. What should we do next?"

"Everything. Dinner. Concerts."

"That sounds good, but one of the reasons I don't want to have a real relationship is Chloe. I don't have a lot of time, and I need to be with her."

"That goes without saying. She should definitely be a part of the plan. And I would like to teach her how to ride. We should spend more time on the ranch together."

"If you're sure."

"I am." He was surer of that than he was about anything else in his life. He wasn't ready to let Alexandra out of his life.

"I need to put Chloe to bed. Do you want to stick around, or do you have to get back to the ranch? One thing I've learned from being around you is that your day starts pretty early."

"I could say the same about yours."

"True. But that doesn't answer my question. Are you staying or leaving?"

"Staying. Definitely."

"Make yourself at home."

He nodded and sat on the couch. He didn't plan on staying long. Just long enough to get a few kisses. Despite how well dinner had gone, the date wouldn't feel like a success if they didn't make out for a few minutes. Alexandra was rolling back the clock and turning him into a horny teenager.

"I hope that didn't take too long," Alexandra said a few minutes later as she returned to the room and sat beside him.

"Not at all."

"Chloe had a good time today. Your family was so wonderful with her. You were wonderful with her."

"She's a sweet girl." Nathan realized that simple statement didn't come close to expressing what he felt for Chloe. That little girl had stolen his heart.

"I like her."

"And what do you feel about me?" he asked, moving closer to her.

"It would be easier to show you than to tell you."

"By all means, go ahead."

Alexandra gave him a flirtatious smile a mere second before she touched her lips to his. The kiss was soft, and he forced himself to let her take the lead. Gradually she increased pressure and then licked his lips. And that's when he lost control. He pulled her onto his lap and then deepened the kiss. The idea of taking this further crossed his mind, but the key in the door stopped him. Alexandra froze and then slid from his lap. They were straightening their clothes when Alexandra's aunt stepped into the room.

She looked at them and a wicked smile crossed her face. "Carry on. I didn't mean to interrupt your evening."

Nathan looked at Alexandra and then stood. "I was actually just saying good-night."

"Yes. We each have to get up early in the morning," Alexandra added, jumping to her feet.

"If you say so," Rose said. "I'm headed to bed myself. Good night."

With that, she turned and walked away. Nathan and Alexandra looked at each other and then burst out laughing. The sexual tension between them dissipated, but he knew with the least bit of encouragement, the fire could be restarted.

"I guess I should get going," he said reluctantly. Leaving Alexandra was becoming harder and harder.

"I know."

They walked to the door together. Nathan caressed Alexandra's cheek. "I'll talk to you soon."

"I'll look forward to that."

He jogged down the stairs and then got into his car. Before he drove away, he looked at the house, pleased to note that Alexandra was still standing in the doorway, watching as he drove away.

Even so, leaving her behind was still painful.

## Chapter Fifteen

"I have some news," Nathan said, excitedly.

"I can probably guess," Alexandra said, leaning against the pillow and adjusting the blanket. Chloe was asleep, Aunt Rose was in her room, and Alexandra was relaxed. She had been looking forward to their nightly conversation all day. There was something so intimate about talking with him in the quiet of night. "You have scheduled your meeting with James O'Brien, CEO of OB Marts. I know you've been after a deal with them for a while, to carry Montgomery beef. How many do they have again?"

He laughed. "Fifty. And you have a better memory for detail than I do. Heck, I should take you with me."

"When is it?"

"This Saturday. We're having dinner."

*Wait. What? He couldn't be serious.* "But this Saturday is Chloe's birthday party." She struggled to keep the panic from her voice.

"I know. But the party is at noon. My dinner isn't until seven. That gives me plenty of time to take pictures and push kids around on scooters. Or whatever happens at parties for one-year-olds before the cake and ice cream."

Alexandra blew out a sigh of relief. Though she and Nathan weren't officially dating, you couldn't tell it from their lives. They spent as much time together as she had with guys she'd actually been dating. They also shared the big and small events of their days with each other. Chloe loved Nathan and had gotten attached to him. He had become an important part of her life. She would notice if he wasn't at her birthday party. Even if she didn't notice, Alexandra would.

It was too late to go back and undo their fake dating scheme. They had grown too close. Their lives were now intermingled. Though she could tell herself that she had no right to expect Nathan to attend the party, she didn't believe that. They might not have talked about it, but their relationship had changed. It was no longer simply pretend. It was real.

"I'm glad."

Nathan's voice became deeper. Softer. "I won't disappoint Chloe. Or you. You both mean too much to me."

Her heart warmed at Nathan's words and the sincerity she heard there. "Thank you. Now tell me more about your meeting."

"We have worked out just about every detail. All we need to do now is sign the contracts."

"Congratulations. I know how hard you worked for this."

"It has been worth it. I am so happy to see the beginning of my five-year plan coming together."

"Your father must be so proud of you."

"He is."

Alexandra knew how much Nathan admired his father. It was clear from the sound of his voice how much making his father proud meant to him. "I'm proud of you too."

"Thank you. Only three days and the biggest deal of my life will be wrapped up."

They talked a few more minutes before they ended the call. Once they hung up, Alexandra set the phone on the bedside table. Now her day was complete and she could sleep easily. That thought had her bolting upright. She should be able to function without talking to Nathan. So why had she thought that? It didn't take long to come up with an answer.

She was in love with Nathan. The thought nearly stopped her heart. She pondered it for a moment and then realized that it was true. She didn't know how or when, but she had fallen in love with him. For a moment she didn't move. Barely breathed as she waited for the panic to hit her. It didn't come. Perhaps because Nathan was the type of man that she could trust with her heart.

He cared about friends and strangers alike. He loved and respected his family. Most of all, he loved

Chloe and was wonderful with her. For the first time in a long while, she believed that it would be okay to love a man. More importantly, she believed it was okay for her daughter to love Nathan. There was no fear that he was unworthy of their love.

But uncertainty remained. Just because she had fallen in love didn't mean that Nathan had too. For all she knew, he was completely happy with the status quo. Although their relationship felt real to her, it didn't necessarily mean it felt real to him. It could all still be a charade to him.

Her heart ached at the thought. The truth was, she wouldn't know how Nathan felt unless she asked him. Since it was bound to be an emotional conversation— at least on her part—it would be best to have the conversation after Chloe's party and after he'd sealed his business deal.

That decided, she rolled over to go to sleep. The past couple of nights, she'd dreamed of Nathan. If she was lucky, he would make an appearance tonight.

The next day was busy at work, but she still managed to finalize arrangements for Chloe's party. Alexandra had invited the five children in her group at day care as well as Nathan's nieces and nephew. Everyone had responded to the invitation in the affirmative. Chloe's first birthday party was going to be a hit.

Alexandra's family would be arriving the Friday before the party. They had already sent a stack of presents ahead, but she had no doubt that they would be bringing even more with them. They hadn't seen Chloe in a while and Alexandra knew they were going to cram several months' worth of spoiling into a weekend.

Alexandra hadn't mentioned Nathan to her family. At the time she'd agreed to be his pretend girlfriend, she hadn't expected it to last this long or to feel this real. Now she was conflicted and unsure how she should introduce him to her family. It would have been simpler to introduce him as her friend if she hadn't invited his nieces and nephew to the party. But she had. Jillian and Savannah would be at the party. If Savannah described Nathan as her friend, that could raise suspicions. She didn't want to ruin things for Nathan simply to avoid a few questions from her family.

Nathan was bringing over dinner tonight, so hopefully they could come up with a solution that worked for both of them.

Nathan stood in front of the selection of toys, unsure which one to buy for Chloe. He'd narrowed his choices down to the final three. Each was different but had something that appealed to him.

"How long do you plan on standing here?" Isaac asked.

"As long as it takes."

"All of the toys you have are good," Miles said. "And take it from someone who knows. She'll probably play with the box and paper a lot longer than the toy anyway."

"Benji might have done that, but Chloe will know that the toy is the gift."

His brothers looked at each other and laughed.

Then Isaac smirked. "Of course she will."

"Why did I even ask you two to come with me?"

"I don't know. Why did you?" Isaac said. "Oh, I know. Because you had no idea what to buy. But if you're going to ignore our expert advice, we can just leave. After all, we have the gifts from our kids."

"You can't go wrong with any of them. So choose one," Miles said. "She'll love it and never know which toys you left behind."

Nathan knew that. "Give me a second."

"We'll go pay for ours," Miles said.

Nathan shooed them away and then turned his attention back to the toys. He picked up the music box. He knew that Chloe liked music. The exquisite, hand-carved music box wasn't exactly something she could play with. But it could be the beginning of a collection. He could give her one every year on her birthday. He liked the idea, so he placed the music box aside.

Next, he picked up the teddy bear family. The four bears were dressed in regular clothes, but there was the option to purchase fancy clothes for them. He'd selected snowsuits and raincoats for each of them. The bears were all huggable, and he could picture Chloe having fun with them for hours. He set them aside and then picked up the shopping cart toy. Chloe could practice walking while pushing it across the room. It also had shapes in varying colors that she could sort. She would have fun with this for hours.

He decided to get all of them. After all, a girl's first birthday was an important event that should be celebrated. Nathan scooped up all the toys and headed for the checkout. His brothers had made their purchases and were standing at the front door holding their bags. When they saw him, they came over.

Nathan glared up at them, daring them to say anything.

He must be losing his touch because Isaac grinned. "Decided to get them all."

"Yes. Do you have something to say about it?"

"Not to you." He turned to Miles and held out his hand. "Pay up."

"You bet on what I would get?"

"I thought for sure you would only get two," Miles said, digging out his wallet. He pulled out a twenty and gave it to Isaac.

"I knew you would get them all," Isaac said, slipping the money into his pocket.

"How?"

"I have a daughter. Miles is new to having a little girl. He'll soon discover how easy it is to spoil them."

Nathan should probably straighten out his brother and remind him that Chloe wasn't his little girl, but he didn't. He would have to explain about the whole charade with Alexandra, something that he wasn't inclined to do at this point. They had convinced his mother that their relationship was real, so there was no reason for it to continue. They could have the big fight and end things anytime without raising suspicions. He supposed he and Alexandra needed to arrange that for some time in the future. Just not now. Definitely not before Chloe's birthday. And really, there was no rush to break up. A few more months wouldn't hurt anything.

He set his gifts on the checkout counter, grabbed several different rolls of wrapping paper, a birthday card, paid for everything, and then he and his brothers returned to the ranch. After dropping his gifts onto the table in the entry, he headed to the stables. There was still a lot to do before he met Alexandra for dinner tonight. Nathan was grabbing his saddle when his phone rang. He looked at the screen and then hurriedly answered it.

"Mr. O'Brien. How nice to hear from you."

"I'll get right to the point. It's about our meeting Saturday."

Dread instantly filled Nathan. He couldn't believe the deal was falling apart. He inhaled and then calmed. "Yes? Is there a problem with the contract?"

"Nothing like that. We still want to partner with you. I'm certain we can work out the minor details. I'm just not able to meet with you on Saturday evening. Would it be possible to meet earlier in the day? Say, around noon? We could have lunch instead of dinner. That's the only time I'm available for the next few months."

That was during Chloe's birthday party. Hadn't he just thought of how important turning one would be for her? But on the other hand, he had worked on this deal for months. He couldn't walk away from it now. He could always stop in before the party started and give Chloe her gifts. Depending on how long lunch went, he could stop in after. He'd worked too hard to make this deal a reality to walk away now.

"That's fine. I'll see you Saturday at noon."

Nathan leaned back and stared at the ceiling. He knew he'd done the right thing. He just hoped that Alexandra saw it the same way. Since they were having dinner together, he would soon find out.

Although he tried to bury himself in work, a nagging sense of unease was never far from him. Alexandra knew how important this deal was to him. Surely she would understand why he had to miss the party.

He was telling himself that same thing hours later when he stood on her front porch waiting for her to answer the door. The aromas of the pizza, which Alexandra said she'd had the taste for, should have been making his mouth water, but instead his mouth was as dry as a desert. He was sure that once they'd talked, he would be able to relax.

The door swung open and Alexandra was standing there, looking as gorgeous as ever. She smiled brightly. "Come on in. That pizza smells so good."

He stepped inside. Chloe was sitting on the living room floor. When she saw him, she pushed to her feet and held out her arms. Nathan handed the pizza to Alexandra and then picked up Chloe and set her on his shoulders. She instantly pounded on his head, and he winced.

"One of these days you'll learn not to do that," Alexandra said.

"No. Eventually she'll learn not to slap me on my

head. But until that day arrives, I'll get used to having a headache."

Alexandra laughed and Chloe echoed her.

They headed for the kitchen. Nathan set Chloe into her high chair and then grabbed plates from the cabinet. Alexandra poured juice for Chloe and then opened a bottle of wine.

"Where's your aunt?" Nathan asked.

"She has her regular card game tonight. I don't expect her until much later." Alexandra put a cut up slice of pizza on Chloe's plate. "She ate dinner earlier, so I don't know how much she'll eat."

Nathan and Alexandra placed a few slices of pizza onto their plates. Alexandra gave him a bowl filled with colorful salad and then started to eat.

When he only sat there looking at his food, she gave him a puzzled look. "Is everything okay, Nathan?"

He blew out a breath. Even though he wanted to have the discussion, he didn't want to ruin her dinner. Since it was obvious that something was on his mind, he might as well tell her. After all, the problem wasn't going to disappear. "Not exactly."

"Is there anything I can do to help?"

Of course that would be her first reaction. Alexandra was kind to a fault. "Not really. I got a call from James O'Brien this afternoon."

"Don't tell me that he wants to back out of the deal."

"Nothing like that. It's still a go."

"Then what?"

"He can't meet me for dinner on Saturday. He wants to meet at lunch."

"On Saturday?" Alexandra asked.

He nodded. "It's the only time that he will be able to meet for months."

"I see." Alexandra set her pizza back onto the plate. "And what did you say to him?"

"I told him that I would meet. What else could I do?"

"I don't know," she said sarcastically. "Maybe tell him that you have plans that you can't break. That's what I would do."

"I can come over before the party. Or maybe after. Chloe won't notice what time I come and leave."

She looked at him incredulously. "But *I* will, Nathan. And I won't have her be a second thought. If you don't want to keep your promises to her, then don't make them." She jumped to her feet so fast she knocked over her chair.

"You're overreacting here."

"I don't think so." Alexandra picked up the chair and scooted it under the table. "You know, this whole charade has been all about you. I played along and did everything that you asked for. I had a good time too, so I have no complaints about that. But when I need you to do one thing, *one thing* that you promised to do, you don't keep your word."

She was right and he knew it. The guilt souring his stomach made him angry and he lashed out. "This isn't a real relationship. It was simply a pretend relationship to fool my mother. That's it."

The fact that it had started to feel real was immaterial and not something he wanted to even think about right now.

"Is she fooled yet?"

He nodded slowly. So fooled that when one of her friends asked about Nathan, she'd told her that Nathan had a serious girlfriend.

"Good. Then we've reached the part of the charade where we have a big blowup and end our relationship."

"Alexandra, don't be hasty." Panicked, he jumped to his feet and crossed the room, closing the distance between them. "We don't have to end everything simply because of a conflict between a party and a business meeting. Surely we can work this out."

She snatched her hands away from his and then hid them behind her back. She stepped away from him, putting the table between them. The emotional gulf between them was much bigger than the physical one. "Why? Nothing between us is real."

It certainly was beginning to feel real. But he wasn't going to say that now. Especially since his sharing his feelings wouldn't change a thing. He wasn't going to be able to attend Chloe's birthday party. Clearly that was a deal-breaker for Alexandra. He was searching for something—anything—to say that would get them back on track. Nothing came to mind.

Alexandra glared at him. "I think you should leave now. Feel free to frame our breakup in whichever way works best for you. I really don't care."

"Alexandra." He was pleading, but he didn't care. He didn't want her to walk out of his life.

"Just go. Please." Her voice broke on that last word, and he realized she wasn't just angry. She was hurt. She must think that he was rejecting Chloe in the same way that Chloe's father had. He wasn't. But nothing he said now would change her perception. Since Alexandra was struggling to hold herself together, he nodded.

"I'll go," he said softly as he walked away. Alexandra trailed behind him. When he reached the front door, he opened it, stepped outside, then turned to look at her. "I'll call you when I get home. Hopefully I can make you understand."

"Don't. There's nothing left to say."

"There is. This isn't the end."

Alexandra didn't reply. Instead she simply closed the door.

It wasn't the end, he told himself. It couldn't be.

Alexandra leaned against the front door and let the tears come. She didn't know why she hurt so badly. She'd known from the beginning that the relationship between her and Nathan was only temporary. A play they'd put on for his mother. Hadn't she just been thinking that the breakup scene was imminent? She hadn't expected this much pain. Reaching into her chest and literally pulling out her heart couldn't hurt more.

Of course, at the time she'd agreed to this farce, she hadn't been in love with him. Falling in love with him hadn't been even a remote possibility. Now she loved him with her entire heart. But if he couldn't love her and Chloe with all of his, there was no hope for them.

The idea of him not being a part of her life was excruciating. But she had survived worse. She would survive this too.

## Chapter Sixteen

"I need to talk," Nathan said the moment he had both of his brothers on the phone. After leaving Alexandra's, he'd driven aimlessly around Aspen Creek, trying to figure out how things had gone so wrong so quickly.

"About?" Isaac asked.

"Sure," Miles said. "Where are you?"

"I'm about ten minutes away from the ranch. Can you meet me at my house in fifteen minutes?"

"We'll be there," Miles said, speaking for Isaac as well.

"Thanks."

Nathan didn't know what he expected his brothers to say. Maybe nothing. But even if there was only a slight chance that one of them would have a bit of inspiration that could salvage things with Alexandra, it would be worth it. His head was spinning, and he couldn't think straight. Even so, he still believed there was a way to work things out. There had to be.

His brothers' cars were already parked in front of his house when he arrived, and they walked up the stairs together silently.

"What's wrong?" Miles asked the minute they were inside.

Nathan inhaled and then blurted out the painful words. "Alexandra and I broke up."

"What? Why?" Isaac asked.

"When?"

"Just now." He paced into the living room, and his brothers followed. Nathan stood in front of the windows and stared into the dark night. He blinked rapidly, not wanting to break down in front of his younger brothers.

"What happened?" Miles asked after a while.

Nathan turned around and faced them. Neither had taken a seat, so Nathan gestured toward the seating area. Isaac and Miles exchanged looks before they sat down.

"What happened?" Miles repeated.

"We had a fight." Nathan shook his head. He still couldn't believe how quickly things had gone sideways. Never in a million years would he have thought Alexandra would be so unreasonable. She hadn't even heard him out.

"About?" Isaac prompted.

Nathan shoved his hands into his jeans. "You know that I have that meeting with James O'Brien."

"We know. The first of your big deals. We already told you how great that is."

"Dad's pleased too. Anyway, we were supposed to meet for dinner Saturday night. He needed to meet earlier. At noon."

"That's the same time as Chloe's birthday party," Miles said.

"I know. When I told Alexandra I would have to stop by either before or after the party, she got angry." And hurt. The pain in her eyes had been unmistakable. It had hurt him too.

His brothers just stared at him. Neither of them spoke for a long moment. It was as if they were waiting for the other to say something. Miles blew out a breath. "And you blame her? You chose a business meeting over her daughter's birthday party."

It wasn't a question, but Nathan felt like he needed to answer it. "It's not as if I'm ignoring her. I'll see her before the party. Or after. Besides, all of her friends will be there. She'll be playing with them. Well, as much as a one-year-old plays with anyone."

"She might not know now that you chose to put business before her, but years from now when she looks at the pictures, it will be clear that you weren't there," Miles said.

"And Alexandra knows now. She's right to be angry," Isaac said. "You're putting her second. If you expect this relationship to last, you had better fix this."

Nathan looked at his brothers. There was no sense in lying to them. He knew they would keep his secret if he asked. Maybe if they knew the truth, they wouldn't be looking at him as if he were the biggest jerk in the world. He had lost Alexandra's respect. He didn't want to lose theirs too.

"We were supposed to have a fight, I just didn't know it was going to feel like this," he muttered.

"What are you talking about?" Isaac asked.

"You know how Mom started matchmaking. I didn't want to be bothered with it, so I convinced Alexandra to pretend to be my girlfriend. It wasn't supposed to last long. Just long enough to throw Mom off the scent. Then we were going to break up and go our separate ways."

"You expect us to believe that your whole relationship was pretend?" Miles asked. He shook his head. "We saw you together."

"Yes." At least at first. Somewhere along the line it began to feel real. He should have told Alexandra when his feelings had started to change. Looking back, he couldn't pinpoint the moment. It had happened so gradually, sneaking up on him. Now he admitted that fear had also held him back. Alexandra had been crystal clear that she didn't want a man in her life. She didn't have time for romance. If he'd told her how he felt, she might have bolted. He hadn't wanted to risk losing her.

So instead he'd hurt her.

"Then if it was all pretend, why am I here?" Isaac asked. "Why did you interrupt my time with Savannah and Mia? My relationship is real. If you and Alexandra planned on breaking up, why are you so upset?"

Nathan dropped into a chair and then rubbed his hand down his face. "I don't know."

"I do," Miles said. "It's because you're in love with her. And the idea of waking up tomorrow and knowing that she won't be a part of your life is tearing you apart."

"I wouldn't go that far." He couldn't have fallen in love with Alexandra. Yet he couldn't totally discount his brother's words. Not when he'd been coming to believe the same thing.

"Take it from someone who lost years with the love of his life. Don't be an idiot. Tell Alexandra that you love her and beg her to forgive you. And then call O'Brien and tell him that you can't meet at noon. Maybe you can split the difference and meet at four."

"And if he can't?"

"Then either cancel the meeting or get used to life without Alexandra and Chloe."

Alexandra looked around the gaily decorated room and gave a determined smile. Her heart might be breaking, but she would keep up appearances if it killed her. Years from now when Chloe looked at the pictures from her first birthday party, she was not going to see a gloomy mother with eyes red from crying. She was going to see a smiling woman.

Alexandra's family had arrived yesterday, and as expected, they'd spoiled Chloe. Alexandra's father and brother hadn't noticed anything was wrong, but her mother and sister had taken one look at her and known. Alexandra had simply told them that she'd broken up with her boyfriend. They'd hugged her and let her know that it would be all right. Of course it would. After all, how long could a heart hurt when the relationship had been no more real than the flowering garden on the photographer's backdrop?

Nathan wasn't the first man to break her heart, but he would be the last. She and Chloe had been doing fine before they met him. They would do just as fine in the future. He'd called her twice, but she hadn't answered. To her, there was nothing that he could say that would change the situation. Either he was all in or he was all out. She couldn't teach her daughter to accept less than she deserved. Chloe was worthy of someone who would always put her first.

It wasn't as if Alexandra didn't understand how important this business deal was to him. Of course she did. But there would always be one more opportunity. One more customer. With her and Chloe out of his life, Nathan wouldn't have to choose. He could stick with his five-year plan. When Alexandra was strong enough emotionally that she could talk to him without breaking down and begging him to choose her and Chloe, she would tell him just that.

Judging from the message Nathan had left her, that conversation might not be necessary. The first time he'd called, he hung up without saying anything. Early yesterday he'd left a message that he had to go out of town for business. She didn't know why he'd bothered to tell her that. It wasn't as if they were continuing their charade. He no longer had to run his schedule by her.

The doorbell rang.

"Guests are arriving," her mother said, pulling her attention back to the present.

"Thanks, Mom." Alexandra checked her watch. It was only eleven forty-five. But then, perhaps someone was extra eager.

"It's time to get the show on the road," Victoria said.

Alexandra looked for Chloe so they could greet her first guest. Alexandra's father and brother were entertaining Chloe in the backyard while Alexandra, Clarice and Victoria put the finishing touches on the family room.

She opened the front door. And gasped. Nathan was standing there, a stack of presents in his arms. He looked more uncertain than she'd ever seen him.

"What are you doing here?" She'd meant to sound firm, but her voice was only a whisper.

"It's Chloe's birthday."

"Yes. But you have your all-important meeting. Remember?"

"I moved it."

"I thought he could only see you now."

"That was the only time he would be able to meet me here. His return flight was canceled, which was why he'd needed to meet sooner. So I flew out to Tennessee to meet with him yesterday. We signed the contract last night."

"How good for you. I'm happy for you," she said begrudgingly.

"I can tell," he said dryly.

"No really. I am. I know how much that deal meant

to you." It had been more important to him than she and Chloe had been.

"It meant a lot. But not as much as I'd once believed. And certainly not more than you and Chloe."

She wanted to believe that, but she couldn't. "Since when?"

"Since I realized that I didn't want to pretend that we're dating."

Her heart sank. For one moment she'd actually thought... "Well, we aren't pretending any longer so... what are you doing here?"

He looked around and then set the gifts on a nearby table. Then he took her hands into his. "I want our relationship to be real. I want to date you for real."

"For real?"

He nodded. "I love you. I have for a while, but I just didn't know it. I know that probably sounds unbelievable, but it's true. Before we met, all that mattered was my five-year plan. I was happy with just having the ranch in my life. But ever since you and Chloe came into my life, my priorities have changed. The ranch still matters, but it is not everything. You and Chloe are."

"I wish I could believe that. But I can't. I know how much your plans for the ranch mean to you. I don't believe you can change your way of thinking just that easily. Even if you can, I don't want to get in the way of your plans. I may as well admit that I love you too. But sometimes love isn't enough."

"Sometimes it is."

"I need a man who puts me and Chloe first. I don't

want to be selfish, and I know that sometimes business will come first. But not on special occasions."

"I know. It will never happen again." His voice was filled with undisguised desperation. Even so, she heard the sincerity there. "Please give me a second chance."

Nathan held his breath as he waited for Alexandra's response. The past couple of days had been the worst of his life. He couldn't live without Alexandra and Chloe. Oh, his heart would still beat and his body would keep moving. He would go through the motions of living. But he would be dead on the inside.

Once he'd realized that Alexandra and Chloe meant everything to him, he'd known he'd do whatever it took to win Alexandra back. He'd called Mr. O'Brien and explained the situation. Then he'd offered to fly to Tennessee. He'd had to make a few adjustments to his schedule, but it had been worth it. He didn't know why it hadn't occurred to him sooner. If it had, he wouldn't have hurt Alexandra as he had.

"I'm scared," she said. "I want to trust you. If it was only me, I would. But I have Chloe."

"I know. If you don't believe anything else I say, please believe that I love her."

Alexandra nibbled on her bottom lip, a clear signal that she was thinking. Then she glanced at him. When he saw the expression on her face, his heart lifted. "I know Chloe loves you. It would be wrong to keep you apart simply because of my doubts."

"So you'll give me another chance?"

"Just one."

He breathed out a relieved sigh. "I won't need a third."

Nathan opened his arms and Alexandra went into them. He closed his arms around her and breathed her in.

He heard Chloe's excited chatter and turned. Her grandfather, Lemuel was holding her. When she spotted Nathan, she squealed and lunged toward him. Alexandra quickly introduced him to her family. He nodded and smiled. There would be time to get to know them better. But first his little angel was here, ready to celebrate her birthday.

"May I?" he asked, holding out his arms. Before Lemuel could answer, Chloe jumped into Nathan's outstretched arms. Nathan took her and held her against his chest. He'd missed his sweet baby. He brushed a kiss against her cheek and then wrapped an arm around Alexandra's shoulder, pulling her close. She leaned against him and smiled.

His life wasn't going according to his five-year plan. That was fine. Good even.

Life with Alexandra and Chloe was better than any plan he could have come up with.

\* \* \* \* \*

### #3031 BIG SKY COWBOY
*The Brands of Montana* • by Joanna Sims

Charlotte "Charlie" Brand has three months, one Montana summer and Wayne Westbrook's help to turn her struggling homestead into a corporate destination. The handsome horse trainer is the perfect man to make her professional dreams a reality. But what about her romantic ones?

### #3032 HER NEW YORK MINUTE
*The Friendship Chronicles* • by Darby Baham

British investment guru Olivia Robinson is in New York for one reason—to become the youngest head of her global company's portfolio division. But when charming attorney Thomas Wright sweeps her off her feet, she wonders if another relationship will become collateral damage.

### #3033 THE RANCHER'S LOVE SONG
*The Women of Dalton Ranch* • by Makenna Lee

Ranch foreman Travis Taylor is busy caring for an orphaned baby. He doesn't have time for opera singers on vacation. Even bubbly, beautiful ones like Lizzy Dalton. But when Lizzy falls for the baby *and* Travis, he'll have to overcome past trauma in order to build a family.

### #3034 A DEAL WITH MR. WRONG
*Sisterhood of Chocolate & Wine* • by Anna James

Piper Kavanaugh needs a fake boyfriend pronto! Her art gallery is opening soon and her mother's matchmaking schemes are in overdrive. Fortunately, convincing her enemy turned contractor Cooper Turner to play the role is easier than expected. Unfortunately, so is falling for him...

HSECNM1223